TERRENCE CULLEN
164 MEADOWLANE
CLYDE, OH. 43410

Ganelon, called Silvermane, was not even remotely akin to True Men. He was a Construct of the Time Gods, an android superman bred to some unknown purpose by an extinct race of mysterious savants.

With the Illusionist of Nerelon as his tutor and ally, Ganelon had begun a career as a wandering warrior, an adventurer, roaming the vastness of Gondwane the Great, Old Earth's last and mightiest continent, righting wrongs, and battling evil and defending the last remnants of mankind from tyrants and oppressors.

He had fought many battles, overcome many adversaries, and won many honors. He was Hero of Uth, Defender of Kan Zar Kan, a Knight of Valardus, and a Baron of Trancore.

But now he had the honor of being a hostage of the barbarian Ximchak Horde, a prisoner in chains. It was a bitter honor, if such it was.

And likely to prove fatal.

D1560313

LIN CARTER

The Barbarian of World's End

DAW BOOKS, INC.
DONALD A. WOLLHEIM, PUBLISHER

1301 Avenue of the Americas
New York, N. Y.   10019

COPYRIGHT ©, 1977, BY LIN CARTER.

All Rights Reserved.

Cover art by John Bierley.

For Avram Davidson, the Grand Duke of Joppa.

FIRST PRINTING, MAY 1977

1 2 3 4 5 6 7 8 9

PRINTED IN U.S.A.

Contents

Book One:
GANELON IN CHAINS

1. Entering Gompery   9
2. Palensus Choy Observes   17
3. Economics of Zaar   25
4. The Humbling of Silvermane   35
5. A Champion for the Gurkoes   43

Book Two:
THE WARLORD OF WORLD'S END

6. A Chieftain for the Gurkoes   55
7. The Kuzaks Ride North   62
8. Bargon the Kazooli Deduces   69
9. The Telltale Scar   76
10. Duel of the Titans   84

Book Three:
THE GREAT XIMCHAK MIGRATION

11. Economics of Silvermane   93
12. Ong, Posch, and the Petrified City   102
13. The Sleeping Forest   110
14. The Problem in Pardoga   119
15. The Strange Little Men of the Hills   128

Book Four:
THE MERDINGIAN REGNATE

16. Beyond the Marvelous Mountains   139
17. The Rescuing of Ruzara   148
18. The Great God Glugluck   157
19. The Land of Warring Cities   166
20. Ganelon Silvermane Departs   174
    A Glossary of Places Mentioned in the Text   183

Book One
GANELON IN CHAINS

The Scene: The Embosch Mountains of Greater Zuavia; the Thirty Cities of the Gompish Regime, Bernille and Jurago in particular.

The Characters: Ganelon Silvermane, Grrff the Xombolian, Ishgadara, the boy Kurdi; the Warlord Zaar, Wolf Turgo and other Ximchaks; Princess Ruzara and various Gomps.

1.

ENTERING GOMPERY

From north to south a high range known as the Embosch
Mountains extended. Like a great wall these mountains di-
vided the Mad Empire of Trancore in the west from the
Thirty Cities of the Gompish Regime in the east.

The tallest peak in the Embosch range was called Thunder
Troll Mountain. At its foot there was a gap in the mountains
called the Marjid Pass.

Early one morning a war party came riding down the
Marjid and passed over into Gompery with a captive loaded
with chains. It was the first month of winter, in a year of the
last century of the Eon of the Falling Moon,* and snow lay
thickly on the cliffs and crunched frostily under the hooves of
the horses.

Well, they weren't exactly horses, they were orniths. That's
short for *Ornithohippus*, "bird-horse," a sort of wingless
quadruped, covered with white plumage, bigger than an ostrich or an emu. During the long ages between this Eon and
our own times most of the life forms on Old Earth known to

---

* A date equivalent to, roughly, seven hundred million years A.D.,
give or take a few decades.

9

our day had become extinct, or evolved into new species. Orniths belonged to one of these new species.

And so did the members of the war party, more or less. Oh, they were human enough, I suppose, to be classed among True Men. They differed from *H. sapiens* only in minor degree. They were chocolate-brown of skin, their bushy beards teased into fat Assyrian ringlets, and tiny gold statuettes representing godlings of their savage pantheon dangled like earrings from pierced lobes. Their main point of departure from True Humanity lay in their eyes, whose irises were of a brilliant scarlet, which they emphasized by painting green circles around their eyes.

These men wore leather helmets horned with Youk antlers. They covered their bodies with heavy-lacquered leather tunics slit up the sides, with short flat-skirts in back and in front. Their bare legs were bound in criss-cross gaiters made of supple leather thongs some two inches wide.

To sum it up, they were bowlegged, dirty, broad-shouldered, smelly, long-armed, and bloodthirsty. They were warriors who belonged to an immense army called the Ximchak Horde, and they were Barbarians.

Their leader was a young man called Wolf Turgo. He was taller and straighter of leg than most of his kind, rather more civilized than his brethren, and somewhat more likable. His gleaming brown body, under his iron-gray furs and polished tunic of lacquered leather, was strong and virile. His lean features were clean-cut, glowing with health and vigor, and even handsome in a wolfish way, despite his feral scarlet eyes.

He had an air about him that was appealing, did Wolf Turgo. He was reckless, energetic, devil-may-care, laughing, mischievous. And he had a sense of humor, even, perhaps, a sense of honor.

But he was a Ximchak, for all of that. And the Ximchaks were the enemies of civilization, haters of cities, destroyers of nations, looters and plunderers.

Ganelon Silvermane did not approve of Ximchaks. He was the man in chains, the captive being carried over into Gompland, which the Ximchaks had conquered and were currently occupying. He had come into this part of the world to fight the Ximchaks, if necessary, and to defeat or destroy them, if possible.

They had taken him prisoner, but they had not captured him. He had surrendered to them to save his friends, Grrff the Xombolian and Ishgadara the sphinxess, from being slain. The Ximchaks had carried these two off into Gompia after Ganelon had soundly defeated them at the Battle of the Ovarva Plains with the assistance of another friend, Palensus Choy, a celebrated magician who owned A Flying Castle called Zaradon.*

Ganelon was a young giant, superbly muscular, like a heroic statue of a gladiator cast in bronze. He was a couple of feet taller than the Ximchaks, and outweighed them by a hundred pounds or so. His magnificent physique was bared to the wintry winds, clad only in a war harness of black leather and boots.

His enchanted weapon, the Silver Sword, was carried by Wolf Turgo.

His face was clean-shaven, heavy-jawed, grim and expressionless. He was not unhandsome and women were attracted to him, although he usually ignored them. His most peculiar feature was his long unshorn mane, which flowed down his back like a cataract of glittering metallic silver tendrils. By this alone you might have guessed him for a Nonhuman.

In fact, this Ganelon, called Silvermane, was not even remotely akin to True Men. He was a Construct of the Time Gods, an android superman bred to some unknown purpose by an extinct race of mysterious savants.

He had passed unguessable ages in a stasis, imprisoned in a Time Vault beneath the Ruined City of Ardelix at the southern end of the Crystal Mountains. From this he had emerged into the world fully grown but with the mind of a newborn infant. An itinerant Godmaker and his wife had adopted him. He had been raised in a city called Zermish, down south in the Hegemony, and had first displayed his heroic nature in the Battle of Uth, when the Zermishmen had routed a herd of Indigons. Ganelon had, in the classic phrase, snatched this victory from the very jaws of defeat.

* See my redaction of the Third Book of the Gondwane Epic, a volume titled *The Immortal of World's End*, for an account of these events.

This had brought him to the attention of the Illusionist of Nerelon, the most powerful magician in those parts, who became Ganelon's mentor and foster-parent. With the Illusionist as his tutor and ally, Ganelon had begun a career as a wandering warrior, an adventurer, roaming the vastness of Gond-wane the Great, Old Earth's last and mightiest continent, righting wrongs and battling evil and defending the last remnants of mankind from tyrants and oppressors.

It was at this time some two years and ten months since Ganelon had emerged from the Ardelix Vault fully grown and in possession of remarkable powers and abilities, most of them still unknown.

By now he had fought many battles, overcome many adversaries, and won many honors. He was Hero of Uth (by Hegemonic Proclamation), Defender of Kan Zar Kan (by Decree of King Yemple), a Knight of Valardus, and a Baron of Trancore (for his part in defeating the attempted Ximchak invasion).

And now he was a hostage of the Ximchaks. The honor, if it *was* an honor, was a bitter one.

And likely to prove fatal.

Beyond the mouth of the Marjid Pass stretched snowy fields and meadows; beyond this a stone-paved post road led past farms and orchards to the gates of the city of Bernille.

The orchards were mere fire-blackened stumps, and the farms had been trampled into mud, the houses and barns gutted by flames. The Ximchaks had conquered this country easily. Too easily, in fact, to please them. The Gomps were a peaceable, wealth-loving people who did not maintain a standing army. That meant that when the Ximchak Horde came pouring down through the northern Xuru Pass into Gompish territory, they were virtually unopposed.

The Ximchaks, however, loved to fight and kill and burn and loot and ravish. These pleasures were, for them, the main reasons for invading in the first place: they were not interested in treasure, really, and did not conquer nations in order to rule them. They just enjoyed fighting and the rest of it, especially the part about killing and burning. So, even though victorious, they had ridden the length and breadth of Gompery killing and burning. Whole cities they reduced in this manner before their appetites were sufficiently glutted.

Bernille was one of these. For centuries it had guarded the Gompish end of the Marjid Pass, extracting juicy tolls from visitors and travelers, and milking fat fees and tariffs from merchants and caravans. Now it was largely in ruin, the mansions and palaces and villas of the wealthy Bernillese—the wealthy were the nobility of Gompland; they had no other conception of an aristocracy—mere heaps of sooty rubble, the streets choked with debris, the walls leveled. Scattered clumps of civilians still eked out a meager starveling existence in their hovels, but most had fled farther south, to the unleveled cities. The Ximchaks mounted a garrison in Bernille, but not a very large one.

Wolf Turgo led his men in through the gates by mid-morn. By some quirk of Barbarian humor, the gates were still standing, even though the city wall had been torn down. Stabling their orniths in the vast echoing marble hall of what had once been the palace of the reigning plutocrat*—now roofless and filled with heaps of dead leaves, and garbage, and snow—the Ximchaks built a fire out of smashed furniture and began to make lunch, while Wolf Turgo went off to find the Ximchak in charge of the local garrison.

They ignored Silvermane, once they had roughly helped him to dismount from his ornith. Originally, they had been intimidated by him, by his sheer physical size, and by the reputation earned by his prowess. But he had submitted to their chains and to their verbal abuse meekly, and his behavior during the journey thus far had been docile. They were beginning to relax around him and ceased regarding him with as much wariness as before.

As for physical mistreatment, well, they had vented a portion of their wrath upon him when first he had surrendered.

---

* The wealthiest man in each Gompish city ruled that city, until another Gomp somehow became wealthier than he, whereupon the previous ruler was deposed in favor of the new. The ruling plutocrat was known as the Regulus. The office was heriditary in the sense that each Regulus generally left all of his wealth to his son, thus ensuring that the Regulusship would continue to be held by his line for at least the next generation. But sometimes two or three wealthy houses would merge, thus creating a plutocrat richer than the Regulus; thus a new dynasty could succeed the old. Odd people, the Gomps; but their system worked.

But Ganelon had endured the buffetings to which he had been subjected with stoicism, neither complaining nor fighting back nor, in fact, seeming to feel the blows, and after a time they had wearied of this sport. Even bullies take little pleasure in slapping around someone who ignores and does not seem particularly discomforted by the said slapping around.

It is not the mere fact of inflicting pain that is pleasuremaking to the bully, it is being the cause of fear. Such people enjoy seeing their helpless victims squirm, cower and whimper; Ganelon did none of these things: hence he soon ceased to be interesting to them in this regard.

Ganelon, once down from the saddle, seated himself upon a fallen block of masonry and contemplated the future grimly but uncomplainingly. For himself, he cared little: he was not a True Man and regarded his fate with something resembling indifference.

His thoughts were upon his comrades, Grrff, the Karjixian Tigerman, and the lady sphinx, Ishgadara. Their condition concerned him keenly. He believed himself in a way responsible for the fact of their captivity, and worried over what might become of them. In particular, he regretted that the Tigerman had been taken prisoner. During the months they had been friends, ever since that first meeting in the arena at Shai, he had enjoyed his rough-and-ready comradeship with burly, uncomplaining, brave and loyal Grrff. To think that the Xombolian now faced a cruel death because of him caused Ganelon great worry and a sense of guilt he had not known before.

He could not imagine a future in which the bluff, swaggering Tigerman no longer stood shoulder to shoulder with him, protecting his back in a fight.

If they killed Grrff, he swore in his heart he would destroy the Ximchaks to the last man. Somehow ...

After a time, he dozed.

After a while, Wolf Turgo returned, having located the garrison chief sporting with some female Gomps. The fellow promised to dispatch a messenger to the Warlord in Jurago, the Gompish capital, without delay. Mounted on a fresh ornith, the herald would reach Jurago days before the more slowly moving war party. Soon Zaar would be apprised of the happy news that Ganelon Silvermane was the prisoner of the Horde—Silvermane, the Southlander champion who had led, or at least had partaken in the leadership of, the forces which had smashed the Ximchaks at Valardus, at the attack on Mount Naroob, and on the bloody Ovarva.

The Warlord would be—pleased.

Wolf Turgo's mouth twisted slightly at the thought. Hardened though he was, the young warrior repressed an inward qualm. He knew all too well the sort of things which pleased his master, and they were not the wholesome things that give pleasure to ordinary men.

He rather liked the bronze giant with the glittering argent mane, did Turgo.

It was a pity . . . but it was war, a harsh struggle for survival, and Wolf Turgo was a Ximchak: to such as he, all non-Ximchaks were the enemy. And in wartime, the enemy is never quite completely human, and any atrocity can usually be justified.

He strolled over to where Silvermane dozed, and prodded him with the toe of his buskin. The huge youth came awake, regarding his captor stolidly, incuriously, and without fear.

"Sent word off to Zaar, telling him we have you safe and sound," said Turgo offhandedly.

"And my friends?"

Turgo shrugged.

"Safe and comfy, as far as I know," he said. "It's you the Warlord wants, not the cat-man or the lady lion. You."

"I know," said Ganelon.

"We'll be mounting up and moving on within the hour, so get some rest if you can. Did my boys give you any food?"

"No."

A curious gleam of something like admiration came and went in the scarlet eyes of the Ximchak captain.

"And of course you didn't ask for any," he remarked. It was not a question. Ganelon said nothing.

"Hoy, Yargash!" Wolf called to his lieutenant. "Some food and a drink of that wine you're guzzling for our prisoner."

The other, a bushy-bearded lout, grinned and stretched.

"Ah, Wolf, what's the difference? Ol' Zaar'll have his guts out to dry ina sun before he has a chance t' digest th' first bite o' chow—"

15

"Maybe," grunted Turgo shortly. "But until then he's in my charge, and gets as good as we get. See to it: I don't want to have to tell you again."

Yargash began to protest, but let his grumblings subside as he caught the look in his captain's eye. Without further ado he cut off a slice of meat, grabbed up a piece of black bread and a leather cup of sour red wine, and brought them over to where Ganelon sat, loosening the bonds on his wrists so that he could use his hands enough to feed himself.

Yargash did not approve of coddling captives, but knew his chief well enough to be wary of rousing his anger. Sometimes he wondered if Wolf was Ximchak through and through; the young officer, at times, displayed a most un-Ximchak civility and concern for others, and something dangerously close to a kind of chivalry.

Then it occurred to him that, after all, a well-fed captive in the full possession of his strength lasts longer under the torture hooks and affords a more vigorous and exciting spectacle. He grinned, a nasty leer: Zaar did enjoy watching um squeal and wriggle under the knives. Maybe Turgo wasn't going as soft as it seemed.

"Eat it up, big man," he sniggered. "Th' stronger you be, the louder you'll yell when the knives be out an' workin' on ya!"

Ganelon said nothing by way of reply to the taunt, and didn't even bother to notice him.

Yargash's grin went sour. He snarled an oath and went off to see to the orniths.

Just past midday the war party remounted and rode out of ruined Bernille, crossed the fields of frozen mud that had once been the rich farms whose produce had fed the populace of the city, and took the stone road east under a grey and heavily-overcast sky.

Some time later they arrived at Jurago, where Zaar the Warlord reigned in the palace of the Gompish monarchs.

Ganelon looked up as they rode in, and looked at the westering sun.

He thought it quite likely he would never see that sun rise or set again. But he did not fear.

2.

PALENSUS CHOY OBSERVES

To the west of the Embosch Mountains lay the country called the Mad Empire of Trancore. Once mighty, it was now virtually powerless. It was ruled by the Gray Dynasts: faced with imminent invasion by the Ximchaks, they had dispatched an aerial embassy to Zaradon, imploring the assistance of the powerful, friendly magician, Palensus Choy.

That was sixteen days ago; today there were no Ximchaks on this side of the mountains. No live ones, at any rate; but there were plenty of dead ones bestrewing the trampled turf of the Ovarva Plains, now buried under the snowfalls.

The city of Trancore was built on an island in the midst of the Greater Pommernarian Sea, which lay directly west of Thunder Troll Mountain and the Marjid Pass. Between the shores of this inland sea, and the foot of this mountain, extended the level grasslands called the Ovarva. To the north there rose a densely wooded tract of forestland known as the Urrach. Along the southern edges of this stand of trees there now stood a most peculiar structure.

It was a castle: a cluster of slim, tapering minarets, carved from glittering white quartz, its domes and roofs plated in cinnabar-red.

17

It was, in fact, Zaradon itself. The famous Flying Castle had easily negotiated the many leagues that stretched between Mount Naroob and the Ovarva Plains, and had swiftly and summarily routed the invaders.

When you possess a castle weighing tens of thousands of tons which you can put down anywhere you like, it becomes a remarkably effective instrument for the disposal of unwanted Ximchaks.

Resident within this remarkable edifice was a tall, thin, amiable and rather absent-minded magician named Palensus Choy. As well, the castle housed two guests, a fat, quarrelsome inventor, named Ollub Vetch, and a little boy named Kurdi. Kurdi was a gypsy boy, one of the Iomagoths who lived in Kan Zar Kan amidst the Purple Plains. He had left home to go adventuring with Ganelon Silvermane and Grrff the Xombolian, serving as Ganelon's squire. When the young giant had voluntarily gone into Gompland as a prisoner of the Barbarians, he had left little Kurdi behind to be taken care of by Palensus Choy.

These persons were, some four days after Ganelon Silvermane's departure, sitting in the great together in the small, cozy parlor of Zaradon, off the great Hall.

The skinny old magician was seated in his easy chair, sipping a mug of hot cider, staring absently into the flames that flickered on the stone hearth. Fat, red-faced Ollub Vetch sat hunched over on the settee, gloomily contemplating the acid burns in his laboratory smock. As for little Kurdi, he was curled up in the window seat, looking out at the falling snow whose fat, soft flakes pattered gently against the lozenge panes of the tall windows. For a time nobody spoke: the flames crackled and sizzled and popped upon the hearth; gusts of wind whistled about the eaves and rattled the windowpanes; from a distant quarter came the clank and clatter of dishware as Chongrilar the Stone Man busied himself in the kitchens.

Then Ollub Vetch cleared his throat and broke the silence.

"Hem!" the fat inventor hemmed. "Anything new happening—*you* know—over thetaway?" He nodded in the direction of Gompland.

Palensus Choy glanced surreptitiously in Kurdi's direction to see if the boy was listening, then said in low tones that he had looked into his vision-crystal that morning, without discovering anything. "They seem to have taken our friend to Jurago, where the Warlord lives. The Barzoolian Palace, I believe. There are wards about the palace, you know, which prevent scrying beyond the curtain-wall."

Vetch wrinkled up his brow distastefully, as he usually did when magic was mentioned: there existed an old, still very lively, feud between himself and Choy as to the relative merits of sorcery and science.

The two continued to chat for a time *sotto voce*, so as not to catch Kurdi's ear. The little boy had taken Ganelon's surrender to the Ximchaks and his present captivity very hard. Indeed, he was inconsolable.

After a time, Choy's major-domo and general factotum, Chongrilar, came to fetch the lad. While the kindly Stone Man lumbered off to give Kurdi his bath and to tuck him into bed for the night, the magician and the inventor talked on into the wee small hours of the night, before going to bed themselves.

For the first three days since Ganelon had departed in chains, in Wolf Turgo's war party, Palensus Choy had observed his journey into Gompery from afar, by magical means.

In his tower observatorium, throned in his Power before the huge scrying-crystal, he had looked on as Turgo led his troop across the Ovarva Plains, fording the shallow floods of the Wryneck River, through the low foothills, and through the Marjid Pass which curved about the thick base of Thunder Troll Mountain.

He had watched them riding down the caravan route and into the ruined city of Bernille. Later, he had looked on as they had emerged from Bernille and, taking the stone-paved post road, had ridden east for Jurago.

Past ruined farms and trampled fields, they rode; past burnt-out houses and the blackened shells of country villas, straight for the Gompish capital. At night they had made camp by the side of the road; with dawn they rose, climbed into their saddles, and continued on their journey, venturing ever deeper into Gompland.*

Despite the heavy, the almost continual, snowfall, Wolf's band made good time on the road. By evening of the third day since taking Silvermane captive, the band entered the gates of Jurago, rode across the half-ruined capital, and entered the barbican gate of the royal Barzoolian Palace.

At that point, as Palensus Choy had already explained to his fat friend, Vetch, he lost the image in the crystal. Court wizards in the service of the Regulus Plutarchus had shielded the imperial abode from all wizardly observations by setting into place magical wards. These nullifying, protective talismans incapacitated the scrying-crystal. Beyond them his magically augmented vision could not penetrate.

Thus, the fate of Ganelon Silvermane remained unknown to his friends in Trancore.

Perhaps it was better so. They could not aid or assist him in his present difficulties, because of the vows of noninterference they had sworn before Wolf Turgo, so it would have been unnecessarily painful for them to have watched the destruction of their mighty friend.

Ganelon had given himself up to the Ximchak hordesmen in order to protect Ishgadara and Grrff from being killed. Part of the deal was that the Flying Castle was to remain where it was now situated, with Palensus Choy promising not to enter Gompland with aerial Zaradon: in return for this, Turgo had sworn that the Barbarian hordesmen would not again enter Gray Dynast territory, or lay siege to Isle Trancore, and would respect the territorial integrity of the Mad Empire.

There is a name for such arrangements:
Stalemate.

By the fourth day after Ganelon departed out of Trancore as a Ximchak prisoner, and vanished from the ken of his friends into the Barzoolian Palace in Jurago, it was obvious that the danger to Trancore had passed and there was no

---

* The Gompish Regime is entirely circled by mountains and is on the border between Greater Zuavia to the west, and its sister-Conglomerate to the east, Lesser Zuavia. Gompia occupies about as much land territory as does modern France.

longer any need for the Flying Castle of Zaradon to remain on the Ovarva Plains, guarding the approaches to the capital of the Emperor Scaviolis.

Nevertheless, Zaradon remained where it was.

It was not exactly impossible, reasoned the absent-minded but acute Immortal magician, that the Ximchaks were not to be trusted, and could not be counted upon to obey their sworn word.

Despite the mutual agreement, the moment Zaradon had flown back to its place atop Mount Naroob in the Iribothian range, who was to say that the Horde might not launch a second invasion of Trancore?

Besides, there was his pet Gynosphinx, Ishgadara, to worry about. Choy was not willing to abandon her to the dubious mercies of these Barbarians—to say nothing of Silvermane, himself. In the weeks they had been friends and fellow-adventurers, the Immortal of Zaradon had conceived of a warm, paternal fondness for the stalwart Champion of Zermish. He would linger for a time on the Ovarva Plains, he had decided, to see the eventual outcome of these affairs.

So he stayed.

But Kurdi didn't.

The little gypsy boy had, after all, overheard the whispered exchange of conversation between Ollub Vetch and Palensus Choy.

Kurdi had taken it very hard that Ganelon had deserted him. The little Iomagoth had been an orphan for as long as he could remember. King Yemple, the kind-hearted and jovial monarch of the Iomagoths, had pitied the bright, inquisitive, lovable child, making him the royal page. But Ganelon was the best friend he had ever had, and the closest thing to a father he had ever known, and the little boy loved him with all the love in his heart.

All he could ask from life was to be near his giant friend, even in adversity.

So, that same night they had chatted together in the parlor before the crackling hearth, with fat snowflakes splattering against the lozenge panes, Kurdi bundled together his few belongings into a leather knap, donned warm suede boots, snug leggings, and a coat of heavy furs, slid down from his window on a rope fashioned from knotted-together bedsheets, and slunk off into the night in the direction of the Marjid Pass, determined to live or die with his huge friend.

He had no difficulty in fording the Wryneck, for the river was frozen over and the ice, although still thin and newly formed, was still thick enough to support his slight weight.

The howling gale-force wind, which had died to a murmur about an hour before, had swept the pass clear and clean of snow. He traversed the Marjid without difficulty, and descended the westerly slope into Gompland.

And vanished from sight.

Next morning, when Palensus Choy and Ollub Vetch got up, they discovered him missing.

Well, it was Chongrilar's discovery, actually. The little boy generally arose earlier than the two men, and Chongrilar had gotten into the habit of cooking his breakfast quite early, so as to have it hot and ready for Kurdi when he came down.

But this particular morning, Kurdi had not come down at his accustomed hour. The Stone Man, deciding the lad had merely overslept, had planned to surprise him with breakfast in bed. And when he carried the tray into Kurdi's small room, then and only then did he find the boy was gone.

Apprised of this when they awoke, Vetch and Choy hastened up the tower stairs and into the observatorium, and wasted no time in activating the giant crystal. Instructing Peraphazon the Genie of Vision to show them the current whereabouts of the boy Kurdi, they gazed into the crystal with astonishment.

It showed a view of a wintry landscape, swept by snow flurries, under the grey light of a lowering sky.

Down a stone road, sluiced by stinging sleet, a small, bent figure toiled doggedly in the direction of Bernille.

They watched for a long time, saying nothing. For there was really nothing to say.

When at last the small, weary figure circled the outskirts of Bernille without discovery, and dwindled from view in the thickening snowfall, they permitted Peraphazon to retire. The crystal dulled, became opaque.

Fat Ollub Vetch tugged viciously on his handlebar mustaches, clearing his throat loudly, and unnecessarily.

It was either that, or sob openly.

Palensus Choy turned his back to the fat little man and daubed moisture from his eyes, blowing his nose noisily into his kerchief.

Love is the most wonderful thing in the world. Any world.

For the next three days and nights they continued to watch the boy's progress across the breadth of Gompia.

There was nothing they could do to help him, long-distance magic being a contradiction in terms. So they watched—and waited—and suffered agonies of suspense.

The patrols did not catch him, did not even notice him.

This was largely because there were no patrols.

At night, or during the heavier snowfalls, Kurdi crept into whatever crevice or shelter or hiding place he could find. Sometimes he slept beside the road, in a culvert or a drainage ditch, or underneath a bush.

He had nothing to eat but berries, a handful of nuts which the squirrels had missed,* and three biscuits stolen from the supper table.

For water, he licked clean snow.

On the morning of the fourth day, while skirting the suburbs of Jurago, he was seen by a party of yag hunters, ridden down and taken captive, carried into Jurago.

Thereupon he, too, vanished from the ken of Palensus Choy, due to those annoyingly efficient wards about the palace.

Kurdi had taken with him out of Zaradon very few of his possessions. The main reason for this was that he had owned very few possessions.

One thing he had taken along was a hunting knife, given to him by King Yemple as a keepsake and small remembrance, what time he had parted from the Iomagoths.

This knife—it was a poignard, really, and Yemple had taken it from the leader of a band of wandering Quaylies who had sought refuge one night in Kan Zar Kan from a dangerous herd of Indigons in heat—measured some thirteen inches from needle point to ball pommel, and was honed to razory keen sharpness on both sides of the blade.

* Not really squirrels, of course, that species having become extinct before the Epoch of the Stone Trees; actually, small, blue-furred rodents called *frixels*, with ring-banded tails like raccoons.

It was quite a good-sized knife for a little boy like Kurdi, almost a shortsword, to one of his diminutive inches.

Choy and Vetch were glad Kurdi had taken it with him. Grrff had taught the lad how to use it to defend himself, and the boy had become proficient in the employment of the blade.

The two old men thought it very likely the weapon would come in handy sometime.

The only other thing of note which Kurdi had carried away out of Zaradon was the Ukwukluk talisman. This was a small, plump oval-shaped scarab of slick, hard paste, big enough to fit comfortably into the palm of the boy's hand. It bore in high relief the stylized likeness of God Ukwukluk the Dispeller of Delusions, a minor divinity in the Vemenoid Pantheon, and the cartouche of that godling, and it was enameled in the same shade of eye-hurting indigo blue favored by the Mentalists of Ning.

Awhile back, the absent-minded magician had employed the powers of this talisman to penetrate the mental illusions of the Gray Dynasts. Later, he had let Kurdi play with it, and had even taught him how to use it.

On the one side, under the stylized likeness of the godling, certain magical characters were cut into the hard composition.

The amulet was of no particular worth or value, and Choy did not mind that the little boy had taken it with him.

And—who knows?—maybe it might come in handy, too.

3.

ECONOMICS OF ZAAR

Between Bernille and Jurago, Ganelon saw very few if any of the natives, but when Wolf Turgo led him into the capital and through the streets of the city toward the Barzoolian Palace, he saw crowds of them.

The Gomps were an interesting-looking race, True Men to half a dozen decimal places, but still novel and unusual enough to be unlike anything he had ever seen before.

They had bright red-brown skins, gleaming and richly colorful, with thick, abundant tresses of the blackest, silkiest, healthiest and *longest* hair he had ever seen sprouting from a human pate.

Some of the plutocrats, probably as a token of their rank or prestige, had black manes so long and heavy they required three or four pages or servants walking in a row directly behind them to carry it. Obviously, these Gomps had never had a haircut since the day they were born. The sight amused Silvermane: now he understood the familiar saying, "Proud as a Gomp with a wain-load of hair," which he had heard many times without ever understanding.

They were an odd race, too, in that the men and the

women looked remarkably different, almost like representatives of two different races.

The women had the same red-brown skin, luxuriant black, silky tresses, and bright pure-gold eyes like new-minted coins. But they were, on the average, nearly twice as tall as their menfolk, lithe and limber and long-legged, whereas the males were short, stumpy-legged, remarkably fat, and faintly grotesque in their appearance.

The men had hooked noses, fat cheeks, numerous chins, low brows under fringes of layer on layer of greasy black ringlets. They talked all the time, shrilling like fishwives, waving their arms and gesticulating with their hands. You got the idea that if you bound their arms to their sides, or tied their hands together so that they could not wave them, they would all be struck mute and could only converse, from then on, by sign language.

The common, almost universal, native costume was a brightly colored silk scarf—vermillion, magenta, tangerine, canary, or scarlet—of enormous length and voluminous size, wrapped again and again around the torso, and looped over the left shoulder. Men and women dressed identically.

They had altogether too many gold rings on their fat fingers for Ganelon's taste.

The women were remarkably handsome, he thought.

As you entered Jurago, viewing it from the west, it looked as if the entire city was a blackened mass of wreckage, as Bernille was.

This proved deceptive; only the western quarter had been put to the torch and leveled. The rest of the city was relatively undamaged.

The Barzoolian Palace stood on an artificial hill in the northern parts of the city, walled about and girdled with gardens watered by tiny artificial canals. It was ornate, gaudy, the outer portions covered with mosaics made up of precious gems, colored crystals, and plaques of semi-precious minerals like lapis lazuli, polished agate, carnelian, malachite, and a bright, artificial purple stone called *aargreb*, which was unique to Gompland and the formula for whose manufacture was a carefully guarded secret of Gompish artisans.

You entered the palace by walking down an avenue lined

with malachite monoliths, like the Great Hall of Karnak, but roofless and open to the sky. You had to circle about the base of a truly colossal statue of Barzooly the rich, founding Regulus of the present dynasty, and the wealthiest plutocrat in Gomp history. Eighty-two feet and nineteen inches high, it was carved out of solid ivory—*all in one piece.*

It did not occur to Ganelon to wonder, as so many thousands of other visitors to Jurago had wondered, what sort of animal could possibly have possessed a tooth or horn or bone or tusk that immense. (Even the largest known species of behemoth, *B. giganticus*, now believed extinct, sported tusks only thirty-five feet in length.)

Zaar the Warlord awaited the arrival of Silvermane in the Third Lesser Audience Chamber. Even this edifice, obviously smaller than some of the others, as its name suggested, was built on a scale of imposing grandeur dear to the Gompish taste.

It was so huge you could have stabled a herd of zeppelins therein, with room left over for a couple of locomotives. And the roof was so high up that, now and again, clouds floated in the western windows, drifted across the width of the hall for a while, taking about twenty minutes to traverse it, unless gale winds were blowing, then floated out the eastern side.

No monarch could have looked very imposing in such surroundings. The sheer magnitude of the hall and its furnishings would have dwarfed anything less enormous than a giant.

Still, Zaar managed to look pretty important.

He was dressed entirely in black iron, and wore a jagged crown carved from one single enormous blue-white diamond.

He was impossibly tall, impossibly huge, incredibly powerful. His wrists were as big around as the upper thighs of ordinary men. The vast muscles that bulged at chest and shoulder, and made the strong iron creak and squeal at every movement, made him look strong enough to wrestle elephants to their knees.

There were no elephants left any more, but had there been, he probably could have given them two falls out of three.

He was darker than most of the Ximchaks, so swarthy as almost to be black; and his head was shaven smooth; and he had a grim expression on his cruel, glowering, thin-lipped face which became glum and gloomy as he watched Ganelon Silvermane approach the foot of the throne.

This was because Ganelon was every bit as tall as Zaar, and looked nearly as impressive, although not so heavily muscled.

Zaar had never seen or even heard of another man as big as he was and it hurt his self-esteem. Somehow, he wouldn't have minded it so much had Silvermane been even taller, but he wasn't; they were of exactly the same height. This meant that Zaar was no longer unique, one of a kind.

He didn't like that feeling at all.

Seated beside Zaar, on a smaller, less significant throne, a handsome young woman eyed Ganelon proudly, a little contemptuously, and with considerable curiosity.

This, Ganelon knew, was the Princess Ruzara, the Pretender to the Gompish Throne. Ruzara, with her younger sister, Mavella, were the only survivors of the Gompish royal family. Their uncle Tharzash had held the throne as Regulus Plutarchus until overcome and slain by Zaar's Ximchaks in the Battle of Poison River. The Warlord had permitted the two royal nieces to live, rather than rendering the dynasty extinct, for some quixotic whim known only to himself.

A good long look at Ruzara, however, suggested to mind one possible reason for her survival. That is, she was a remarkably attractive young woman. Her raven hair was sleek as oiled silk, and long as a banner. She had a clear, tanned, healthy complexion, and her eyes were like immense and brilliant golden gems. Her trim, boyish figure, long, coltish legs, and small, firm, pointed breasts reminded him of Xarda, the girl knight of Jemmerdy, who had been among his companions on earlier adventures.

After one good look at her, Ganelon turned his attentions to Zaar and forgot all about the long-legged Gompish girl.

But she continued to study him. Ruzara had seen the young giant in action during the Urrach ambush, and had watched with awe and fascination his amazing battle prowess. Although she had fully identified herself with her Ximchak conquerors, turning from her own people in disgust at their timid, unwarlike ways, and although Ganelon was an enemy of the Ximchaks, she could not help admiring his magnificent physique, and the simple dignity with which he wore his chains.

Zaar was also impressed: but mostly he was annoyed.

He sat upon his throne, glowering down at Ganelon Silvermane, listening with half an ear to Wolf Turgo's account of the method by which the Zermishman had been persuaded to surrender himself.

It was difficult for the Warlord of the Ximchaks to believe that this silent, impassive captive had been responsible for the recent, disastrous string of defeats the Horde had suffered. The honor had been given unto the numerous and powerful Gurko Clan of laying siege to Valardus, of attacking Zaradon atop Mount Naroob, and of the attempted invasion of the Trancorian realm. And at each phase, Ganelon had been there, Ganelon and his handful of friends, to somehow circumvent the Ximchak thrust, destroying them in astonishing numbers.

Some eight thousand two hundred Gurkoes had perished on the Ovarva alone, he recalled grimly. Earlier, before Valardus, the Mobile City of Kan Zar Kan had accounted for another three thousand, while five hundred had died in the attack against Trancore. And something like twenty-six hundred had lost their lives in the ill-fated assault against the Flying Castle of Zaradon atop Mount Naroob.

In all, fourteen thousand, three hundred of Zaar's hardiest warriors were dead, and the mightiest of all the Nine Clans was now reduced to a minor position in the Horde.

And all because of the one man who now stood before him, loaded down with chains, a helpless captive!

It was pleasant to contemplate. The remnants of the Gurko Clan which had survived would be keenly eager to watch the destruction of their principal enemy. Indeed, their Warchief was en route to the Palace at this very moment, to be in at the kill.

When Turgo had finished his account, Zaar sat without speaking, fingering his sword-hilt, musing.

Silvermane said nothing, merely stood there unbent by the weight of his chains. If he tasted fear deep within his heart, at least no sign of this could be discerned in his face.

Zaar frowned, hating him. Because of Silvermane his most powerful Clan, composed of his most loyal supporters, the backbone of his reign, were decimated. In the place of the Gurkoes, a power vacuum now yawned, and the Warchiefs of the other Clans were jockeying and horse-trading to fill it. The highest councils of the Horde were torn by dissension and it might be weeks or even months before things sorted themselves out.

He could kill this prisoner: nothing would be easier. A word—a gesture—and it was done. He could have Silvermane burned alive, or tortured to death, killed by slow inches. This might glut the angry resentment of the surviving Gurkoes, but it seemed to Zaar to be hardly enough.

Death comes to every man: it is the inevitable companion of life. Surely, the enormities committed by this whitehaired giant were such as to require the invention of a truly unique and original doom. . . .

Boots crashed on the tiles. In swept the Warchief of the Gurko Clan, burly, black-bearded Lord Barzik in a flurry of henchmen and subchiefs. Among these were Farrash, his right arm in a sling from hurts taken when he had led the doomed first Hundred over the crest of Naroob; and Black Unggo, whom Ganelon had defeated terribly at the Ovarva; and Larx, Iquanux, and old Harukh Irongrim, the senior tribal chief of the Gurkoes. These bore expressions which boded ill for Ganelon Silvermane. They were hungry for their dead thousands to be revenged. Wolf Turgo unobtrusively took his place among them.

And Ganelon stood alone, ringed in by enemies.

And the judgment began.

The business of a suitable doom for Ganelon Silvermane occupied the Horde leadership over the next two days.

Zaar felt that merely killing Silvermane, even though that death might be indefinitely protracted by slow, lengthy stages, was not enough, somehow. Silvermane must be humbled, humiliated in some dramatic manner.

Lord Barzik tended to agree. When Turgo learned of this unexpected direction the judging of Ganelon was now taking, he felt a surge of elation he was careful not to show. The young Ximchak had conceived a healthy admiration for the big man, and would have been sorry to see him slain.

Black Unggo, however, backed up by his toady, Iquanux,

could conceive of no less fatal punishment than death. The loutish Unggo, a stupid unimaginative bully, had succeeded to the chieftaincy of his tribe when his leader, Red Qarziger, had been killed during the Ximchak assault on the Bryza, as the imperial palace of Isle Trancore was called. Unggo's leadership had, thus far, been a distinctly unremarkable one: he had failed to take the Bryza, failed to hold the siege at all, and been resoundingly defeated on the Ovarva Plains.

The one smart thing he *had* done was, in retreating from the bloody shambles of Ovarva, to carry off Ishgadara and Grrff. Even that, it must be told, was not his own original idea, although he had long since forgotten the fact. The notion had been suggested to him by Harsha of the Horn, a bright, intelligent young Gurko who had overseen the capture of the two.

In the end it was the idea of Wolf Turgo which carried the day.

Turgo pointed out that, to Ganelon, death would be no dishonor, merely defeat. What would truly, and deeply, rankle in the heart of the Zermish champion would be to be forced *to aid and assist* the Horde in further conquests and depredations.

"Make him enlist in the Horde as a common warrior," Wolf urged cleverly. "Force him to lend his gigantic strength and prowess and skill in our wars. *Make him fight against his own former friends and allies—make him help to defeat the very countries he came here to fight us in order to protect!*"

There was a deviousness to this plan that Zaar rather liked; the simple perversity of its twisted logic strongly appealed to his innate cruelty and brought a reluctant grin to his thin lips. He suspected that Turgo was right: this was the one punishment above all that would break the heart of Ganelon Silvermane.

"Death before dishonor" was an obsolete phrase, but the idea was not unknown, even to the Ximchaks. This doom could be termed "dishonor before death," and the poetic irony of it rather pleased the Warlord.

"And, as the ultimate humiliation," added Wolf slyly, "force the big man to join the very Clan he has so heavily defeated and so nearly wiped out. Make him a Gurko!"

"Aye," grunted Barzik ominously. "Give him to us, Lord.

We'll teach him what it means to be a Gurko! Before my captains are through with him, we'll make the dog regret the day he was born!"

Zaar looked the idea over, and could find nothing wrong with it. It was whole and perfect—the most exquisite refinement of revenge imaginable. He looked at Wolf Turgo with a gleam of satisfaction in his eye: the young officer was of the troublesome younger generation of Ximchaks, and they were beginning to display treasonous signs of dissatisfaction with the immemorial ways of the Horde. Some of the polish of the civilizations through whose gory wreckage he had led them seemed to have rubbed off on them; they demonstrated at times a squeamishness, a human tendency toward something almost resembling chivalry, that alarmed him. Turgo he had long suspected of harboring the softer sentiments: it pleased him that the young man was capable of such delicious cruelty as his suggestions for Silvermane demonstrated.

"Let it be so, then, if you wish it, Barzik," he nodded.

"By the way, Lord," murmured Wolf Turgo, "a hunting party recently captured a little boy from Trancore on the outskirts of Jurago. Says he's Silvermane's squire; seems that he followed the big man here in order to be with him. Kid's too puny to make much of a slave, and not worth killing. Shall I toss him in with Silvermane?"

"Why not," shrugged the Warlord, turning his attention to other matters. And so Kurdi was spared.

Wolf soon found a chance to speak privately with Ganelon before he had been summoned before Zaar to hear his sentence of doom.

It was the fact of Kurdi which afforded him that chance, which is probably why the young warrior concerned himself with the child in the first place. He escorted the lad to the cell where they were holding the big Zermishman, gruffly bade the jailer unlock the door, then cut Kurdi free of the choke-halter about his neck and turned him loose.

The little boy squealed, flung himself at Silvermane, and wrapped himself about Ganelon's leg, hugging it tightly and babbling breathlessly. Ganelon regarded his little squire fondly, patted him on the head, and looked beyond him expressionlessly at Turgo.

The warrior shrugged with a sheepish grin.

"Don't blame me, big fellow! This was all the kid's idea, and all his doing, too. He must have followed us, hiding so he'd not be spotted by our sentinels or patrols."

"Is that true, Kurdi?"

"Din' wanna let you go alone," the boy said tearfully. "Ol' Master Choy, he din't know. I snuck out one mornin' ... been follyin' ya f' days—"

" 'Following,' " Ganelon corrected him absently. Then he tousled the boy's unruly black curls and hugged him affectionately. "It's all right, Kurdi: Ganelon understands. Everything will be all right. I won't let them hurt you."

Turgo sidled near, one eye peeled for the guard.

"Lissen, big fellow: Zaar's decided to make you join the Horde, to make you fight against your own friends, rather than just killing you. You gotta go along with the idea—"

Ganelon shook his head wearily.

"I will never fight against my friends; I'll die first," he said. "You know that, Turgo; you know me better than that."

"Sure, sure! But, lissen—it's a way of staying alive for a while longer! Give ya a chance to get away with your friends, maybe. Just play along for the time being. What harm can it do? It's either that, or the knife. A slow knife, at that. Dead, you can't do nothing. Alive ... well, there's always a chance. Take that chance, you big stubborn lummox!"

Ganelon looked at him curiously.

"What does my death matter to you, or my life either, for that matter? You're a Ximchak; we are enemies. Why should you care if I live or die?"

Wolf chewed on his lip for a moment.

"Damn you, I don't want your death on my head," he growled. "Fightin' an army is different than fightin' one man. You can't see their faces, you don't know them as individuals. They are just things in your way, things to be cut down before they cut *you* down. But you, you're different. Don't ask me why! Back there in Trancore, when I was Zaar's ambassador, I got to know you, to, well, like you. Somebody else'll hafta be your death: not me."

It was quite a remarkable speech, coming from a Ximchak.

Ganelon stared at Wolf Turgo unbelievingly. Turgo flushed as if embarrassed to admit himself capable of friendship, then strode out of the cell with a final, brusque admonition.

"Play along with Zaar, for all our sakes!"

That night, while the boy slept the sound sleep of exhaustion, curled up against him, Ganelon lay awake, staring at the ceiling, his mind busy with unaccustomed thoughts.

Ganelon had rarely had to use his wits in the last three years. Always there had been somebody to hand cleverer than he, to decide difficult choices and make decisions: first Phlesco and Imminix, his foster parents; then his master, the Illusionist; finally, Grrff and Choy and Vetch. But now, for the first time, he was alone—on his own—with no one to help him through the choices and decisions. Now he had to do all the thinking.

He didn't like it. Up until now, as well, he had rarely gotten into a tough spot he couldn't smash and bash his way out of, relying on brawn alone, instead of brains: on his warrior skill, rather than his wits.

But he was chained and helpless, in the midst of an army of foemen two hundred thousand strong.* Muscles alone would not suffice to get him out of this situation.

He would have to *think* his way out, or not get out of it at all. He would have to be as devious and cunning as his enemies; he would have to learn patience and humility, to wait and watch and endure, until the chance came for freedom.

The next morning the guards came to drag him before the Warlord.

The sentence of doom was passed upon him.

And Ganelon bowed his head and accepted it.

That day he was sworn by grim vows, shared blood and wine with his captors, and formally renounced his Hegemonic allegiance.

From that moment on, he was a Ximchak Barbarian of the Ximchak Horde.

---

* Actually, the full Ximchak strength at this point was 181,700.

4.

THE HUMBLING OF
SILVERMANE

On the whole, it was rather un-Hordesmanlike of Zaar to use such expediency in his judgment against Ganelon. Generally, the Warlord would have agreed with most of his warriors that the only safe enemy is the dead enemy. But his unusual venture into economical considerations certainly paid off: the bronze giant could do the work of ten men, and could do the fighting for twenty.

Barzik put Ganelon in Wolf Turgo's Hundred, under Black Unggo's chieftaincy. He told Unggo to work him hard and break his spirit. Unggo did his best.

The first week he spent as a volunteer Ximchak, they put Ganelon to digging ditches, cleaning out latrine pits, burying corpses, and doing every other dirty job they could think of. Ganelon did as he was told without murmur, but his gigantic strength and enormous stores of vitality were such that the most backbreaking tasks they could think up for him were child's play. He hardly seemed to feel the exhausting toil, or notice the degrading, filthy jobs he was given.

At first, an audience of leering, grinning Gurkoes was always there to taunt and jeer and catcall and pelt him with garbage. Ganelon stolidly ignored them and did his work, like

Samson in the captivity of the Philistines, except that he was not blinded.

When a bully fails to get a rise out of a victim, he gets surly and sometimes loses his temper. This happened to some of Ganelon's tormentors, and they came down into the pits to slap him around a little. The first one Ganelon picked up and tossed into the latrine pit, where he sank into stinking ooze with an astounded gurgle. The next three were thrown as far as Ganelon could throw them, which was pretty far. They picked themselves up, feeling as astounded as the poor fellow in the latrine, if less dirtied.

In time they would experience a reluctant admiration for their uncomplaining victim, who did the work of a whole squad of men without a murmur. In time this admiration would turn to grudging respect. Also in time, Ganelon's novelty would wear off and he would be just another Ximchak. There were hundreds of recruits from other races among the Horde, outlaws and outcasts and former slaves or war prisoners who had joined the Horde, which seemed invincible.

But that lay still in the future. Ganelon had to swallow a lot of jeers and sniggers before then. He endured his humiliation with a degree of patience he had not known he possessed. After all, he had Kurdi's companionship and the covert sympathy of Wolf Turgo, who stepped in from time to time to prevent a more brutal hazing than a bit of attempted slapping around. He could wait it out, he thought.

And he did.

On several occasions during this period, the Princess Ruzara came riding by to observe the humbling of Silvermane. Sometimes she rode forth accompanied by her sister, Mavella, and sometimes not; but generally she was escorted by Harsha of the Horn, the young herald of the Gurkoes who had conceived of a powerful admiration for the beautiful and warlike Princess, which she scorned.

On the first such occasion, she was dressed in a stylishly feminine version of Ximchak battledress. Her long, trim legs were clothed in tight trousers of forest green, and she wore suede boots and a close-fitting leather jerkin, with a bow and quiver of arrows over one shoulder.

A born tomboy, an adolescent Amazon, Ruzara had adopted the ways of the warlike Ximchaks with wholehearted enthusiasm, the reaction having sprung from the contempt with which she viewed her own people's feeble inability to defend their realm against the invaders. She now identified fully with the Horde.

Her sister, however, was all cool snow and pallid lilies, to her fire and vigor and peppery spice. Mavella was slim and pale, with platinum-blond hair, most un-Gompish a color. Where Ruzara cursed and swaggered like a Ximchak boy, Mavella was reserved and ladylike and fastidious. The Twin Princesses (as they were called) failed to agree on anything, and it had always been thus between them.

Ruzara delighted in loudly bemocking his condition, while Mavella shuddered delicately and averted her eyes from such unclothed masculinity. It should be explained here, perhaps, that Ganelon was knee-deep in a sewage pit at the time, and was covered from head to foot with filth, having prudently removed his garments before beginning the job.

No matter how Ruzara taunted him, she could extract no reaction from the giant, who stolidly ignored her catcalls, and worked away at his unpleasant task.

Eventually, Ruzara rode off in a huff, accompanied by her sister and Harsha. Ganelon pretended not to be aware of their going, as he had failed to respond to her presence.

He had, simply, to endure, and to wait things out.

One thing that made the waiting-out easier was the sympathy and respect of such as Wolf Turgo and Harsha of the Horn, who scarcely bothered to pretend they did not like him.

And, besides, there was Grrff and Ishgadara, not to mention little Kurdi.

The Karjixian Tigerman and the sphinx-girl were of course free now of all constraint, and could return to Trancore whenever they wished.

It is quite possible that the Warlord Zaar might have conveniently "forgotten" his promise to free the two captives if and when Silvermane surrendered himself to Ximchak justice. He might have done this deliberately, or he might have actually overlooked his commitment. At any rate, while his attention was distracted elsewhere, attending to more pressing and urgent problems, the friendly Wolf Turgo had taken it upon himself to give the orders to set them free.

Grrff had lost considerable weight while a prisoner in Gompland, and his bony ribs showed plainly through his dirty fur. But Ganelon found the sight of him, alive and well, a handsome sight indeed. The huge, burly fellow, with his black-and-orange striped fur, prick ears, lashing tail, and heavy, taloned paws looked mighty good to Ganelon. They hugged each other fiercely, blinking back the tears that stung their eyes, slapping each other on the shoulders—an affectionate exchange of buffets hearty enough to snap the spine of warriors less powerful than they.

"Big man," huffed the Karjixian in his hoarse, deep-chested purr. "Ol' Grrff figgered he'd seen you for the last time! Dang shame we gotta meet like this, all these lousy Ximchaks hangin' around; but better this way than never!"

Ganelon grinned until his cheek muscles cracked, trying to keep back the happy tears. To hide his emotion, he poked a thumb in Grrff's furry ribs.

"Guess they haven't been feeding you enough," he observed. The Tigerman uttered his growling laugh.

"Now, that's a fact! Still an' all, this Ximchak swill is a whole lot better'n that stinkin' fish stew they fed us on in Trancore."

Ganelon was happy to see Ishgadara, too. The big sphinx-girl came waddling out of her cage, grinning so broadly as to expose all of her square white tushes, her great full bare breasts swinging. She kept folding and unfolding her vast, bronze-feathered wings with a *snapp!* like a Chinaman playing with his fan.

"Ho, dere, pig man, how you? Cat-poy an Isshy, we jus' apout giffink you up! How fat li'l master an tall skinny master?"

"It's good to see you too, Ishgadara," Silvermane admitted. "Both Palensus Choy and Ollub Vetch are well, although they miss you a lot, of course, and are concerned for your safety. You haven't been harmed, either of you?"

"Not us," growled Grrff, bristling. "Once ol' Grrff let'm have a glimpse of his claws, Zaar's bullyboys gave him a wide berth. Same with Isshy, here: she knocked a hole through a stone wall with one barehanded punch, just to show 'em what's what. After that, they treated her with the respect due a real lady!" The Tigerman grinned fondly at the sphinx-girl, wrinkling his furry snout and revealing a healthy set of fangs.

"I'm relieved to hear it," said Ganelon.

" 'S sure good to see you again, big fella," grumbled Grrff, "but Grrff's sure sorry it had to be like this. You should never of given yerself up to save us, you know. We'da gotten out of this spot, somehow ... but now you're stuck here, too."

Silvermane shrugged, saying nothing and looking a trifle uncomfortable. It always bothered him when people praised him for his valor, his courage or his strength. It seemed, somehow, superfluous. He was not a True Man, only a Construct, and it seemed to him that his life was, or ought to be, of little value. He had been shaped to some purpose still veiled in the mystery of the unknowable future, and those who had molded him had given him the stamina and vitality of a dozen men. His superhuman vigor and valor, strength and skill, were natural to him and he did not like being complimented for them.

So he changed the subject, pointing out that part of the bargain he had struck with Wolf Turgo, on the behalf of the Horde, was to exchange his freedom for that of his friends. Therefore, unless the Warlord intended to renege on the word of his envoy, Grrff the Xombolian and the Gynosphinx were free to leave as of right now. And, to his way of thinking, the quicker the two took advantage of their freedom and flew back to Zaradon and safety, the better. There was no way of telling how long they would be free to do so.

However, neither the sphinxess nor the fur-clad Karjixian would even consider flying to freedom, leaving Silvermane in chains to face an unknown doom. They insisted on staying with him to the end of this, no matter what the end might be.

"Tush, big man," grinned Grrff, making light of the danger. "Ol' Grrff's got nothin' to worry about! A white-eyed Yombok woman told him once, ol' Grrff'd die fat an' happy, and in bed, surrounded by hunnerds o' his grandcubs. So don't *you* be a-worryin', nossir!"

"But, Grrff—"

"You thought enough of us, big fellow, to give up yer freedom for yer friends," growled the Tigerman. "Some friends we'd be, takin' advantage of the chance and leavin' you to take the consequences. Nothin' doin'—we're gonna stick with you. Right, Ishy?"

The sphinx-girl grinned toothily, nodding her huge head in amiable agreement.

"But then it's all for nothing, and we're all prisoners of the Horde," Silvermane protested. "What did I give up my freedom for, if not to give you yours?"

"Wellsir, to ol' Grrff's way o' thinking," said that worthy, "you did it to save our lives, 'cause they wuz gonna kill us, else. Now we're saved; Wolf Turgo sez they ain't gonna kill us no more. Least we can do, in that case, is stick around and be here when you need us. Ishy's wings might come in handy, y'know, when you decide you've had enough of this muck. She c'n fly the both of us outa here, anytime," he added in a hoarse whisper, with a conspiratorial wink.

Ganelon said nothing, only looked more uncomfortable than before.

The fact of the matter was: *He had given his word.* To join the Gurko Clan voluntarily. To take the oath of Clan loyalty without reservation. To never attempt an escape.

Now Silvermane was only a bred-to-order synthetic man, but one thing he had in common with True Men was a sense of personal honor. He clung to it proudly; in that respect, at least, he was human. He would never go back on his word, or break a vow, or betray a comrade.

And he had not the slightest intention of trying to leave the Horde.

But how could he explain this to Grrff or Ishgadara? To have told them that he intended to remain loyal to his Clan oath, come what may, would be like bragging about his sense of loyalty and honor. And it was not in Ganelon to brag about anything.

So he kept silent.

And they stayed with him.

The humbling of Ganelon Silvermane was continued by Black Unggo until it became blatantly obvious even to him that it was not going to accomplish anything.

There's no particular point in overworking a man who doesn't even feel it, or in hazing a man who can't be hazed, or in trying to break the spirit of one whose spirit is unbreakable.

The work details continued until, after a few more days, the Gurkoes no longer came to jeer and snigger and catcall. When they did hang around to watch Ganelon digging ditches, they were reluctantly forced to admire the way he took their taunts with unruffled dignity, and to gawp in awe at his prodigious and untiring strength. It's hard to jeer at a man you admire, so after a while they just stopped coming.

Since there was no point in continuing to expose Ganelon to public humiliation when the public no longer came to humiliate him, the inhuman work assignments were quietly dropped. Silvermane was assigned to a squad tent along with the other Gurkoes, and began to become one of them. But not before he had to pound in the ears of a couple of squad bullies, just to get them to leave him alone.

The other warriors in his squad rather liked him for that, since most of them had suffered a little bullying at the hands of the two Ganelon had so easily succumbed. It's hard not to like someone who mops up the floor with a bully who had been the bane of your existence for a long time—especially when the new top man in the tent makes no attempt to bully *you*.

So Ganelon began to be liked, albeit gingerly, and at a distance, and without anything actually being said about it.

He became accepted.

So did Ishgadara and Grrff the Xombolian and the boy Kurdi.

It seemed bewildering to the chiefs of the Gurko Clan that their former prisoners now wanted to stay on as Gurko recruits, but they couldn't think of a valid or sensible reason to say no to the request. After all, from being the largest and strongest of the Clans which made up the Ximchak Horde, they had recently suffered a drastic reduction in manpower, fighting strength, and with all of the resultant loss of prestige that reduction implied.

When the one thing you really do need is recruits to help build up your strength again, it seems dumb to turn down people who really want to be recruited.

So Grrff and Ishgadara joined the Gurkoes (although with unspoken reservations and fingers slyly crossed behind their backs during the oath-swearing). They were put into Ganelon's squad because nobody else wanted them, and because that's where they wanted to be. Kurdi was allowed to serve Silvermane as his squire simply because there was nothing else they had for him to do.

While the warriors in this particular squad gradually got used to Ganelon Silvermane and Grrff and the Gynosphinx living and working and drilling and sleeping among them, that didn't mean the other Gurkoes failed to seize every opportunity to make fun of them or try to haze them.

So Ganelon had to break quite a few more jaws, as did the Tigerman and the sphinx-girl. The number of lame or limping or bandaged or toothless Ximchaks in Wolf Turgo's Hundred increased in time to such a point that word began to spread among the Hordesmen that it would be wise to take no notice of the new and unusual Gurko recruits.

In time the hazing, or the attempted hazing, petered out.

The Gurko Clan, it seems, had run out of uninjured hazers.

When this came about, Wolf Turgo (who, officially, had taken no notice of the brutal treatment the newcomers were being subjected to, such behavior being customary), breathed a secret sigh of relief.

New recruits in camp always stand out like a sore thumb for a while, he knew: but in time even the most unusual become assimilated, as the other warriors become accustomed to having them around.

Before very long the very same quality of unusualness that made them such tempting bait for hazing became an object of pride to the Gurkoes of Wolf's Hundred.

What other squad could boast of a seven-foot Tigerman with claws like steel hooks, or a bronze colossus who could work or fight like ten men, or, for that matter, the likes of Ishgadara?

She could *fly*.

And theirs was the only squad in the Ximchak army with its own built-in air force!

5.

A CHAMPION FOR THE GURKOES

Winter drew its snowy mantle across the broad valley of the Gomps. The passes which cut through the ring of mountains which circled the Gompish realm became snowbound, making an invasion or even a surprise raid improbable, even impossible.

The Ximchaks relaxed their vigilance.

They also began to grex more than usual.

To grex is a verb uniquely Gondwanish. It means to grouse, gripe, grumble, in a low, indistinct mutter.

Before long, the mutter became louder. In time, it became deafening. Before Ganelon and his friends had been among the Ximchaks three months, the vociferous complaining and surly temper of the Hordesmen became a matter of concern to the leadership of the Horde.

Part of the trouble was that the Horde was made up of warriors, and warriors are never quite completely happy except when they are fighting other warriors.

If they don't have any foreign enemies to fight, they take to fighting among themselves in time. This leads to bad morale and full graveyards. It also leads to longstanding feuds which, unless checked in time, can tear an army apart.

43

And part of the trouble was even simpler and easier to understand: the Horde was *getting hungry*.

You cannot pen a couple hundred thousand warriors and their women and beasts inside any fair-sized country for too much time, before you begin to deplete the resources of that country.

In the case of Gompia, "deplete" would be an understatement. "Exhaust" was more like the *mot juste*.

When the Ximchaks had first come rampaging down through the Thirty Cities of the Gompish Regime, they had burned and looted and raped and pillaged without pausing to take thought for the morrow.

The reason for this was, quite probably, that they had assumed they would soon be moving on. So they had burned the granaries and trampled the fields and flattened the barns and corncribs and set fire to the orchards and slaughtered the herds, and, in general, enjoyed themselves in the immemorial way of true Barbarians.

Then, a while later, wearying of lording it over the subjugated and not very interesting Gomps, they had sent an expeditionary force south through the mountains to scout out some new lands that were ripe for conquest. Marching through the Iribothian Mountains, they crossed the jungles of Nimboland, entered the Carthazians, and laid siege to Valardus.

Here they had suffered the first of a remarkable series of disconcerting setbacks. *Very* disconcerting setbacks. For the Mobile City of Kan Zar Kan had broken the Valardine siege and slaughtered them by the hundreds. Retreating in confusion back to Gompery, they were severely decimated again before the gates of Zaradon. So much, they decided, for the idea of going south.

Then they tried a probe to the west. Gurkoes poured through the pass and encircled Trancore, or tried to. Again, they suffered a devastating setback, for they died in their thousands on the meadows before Trancore. So much for marching west.

Now, east was out of the question, for in that direction lay Xoroth the Fire Desert, where nothing lived or could live. To go north was equally unthinkable, for it was from that direction that they had come in the first place. A Ximchak never retreats (well, hardly ever); and, anyway, in passing down through the north into the Gompish Regime, they had pretty much eaten those boreal realms barren, too.

Thus, it was stalemate.

They just sat there in Gompery, getting more and more hungry, and more and more quarrelsome and bad-tempered.

It was problems like these that had distracted the Warlord Zaar from giving the punishment of Ganelon Silvermane his full and ferocious attention.

He solved them in a characteristically economical way, by making one solution fit both problems.

Zaar decreed that each tribe should hold a series of competitions in athletic ability and battle skills, and that the champions of each tribe should compete for the championship of the Clan; the Clan champions would then compete for the Grand Championship of the entire Horde.

These activities, he reasoned, would siphon off the restless tempers of the Horde, and would give everyone something to watch, an entertainment to divert them from their troubles, and a motive for the rebuilding of tribal and Clan morale in the prowess of their champions.

When the proclamation was read in the encampments of the Horde, centered about the outskirts of the partially ruined city of Jurago, Ganelon at first did not wish to compete. The modesty of the Construct was such that he did not consider it an equal contest to pit his unique strength and vigor against mere men.

Ganelon did not mind fighting, but he did not like showing off.

His new friends among the Gurkoes soon persuaded him to reconsider. It was argued by Wolf Turgo and Harsha of the Horn, by the chieftain Larx and even by old Harukh Irongrim, the senior tribal chief, that Ganelon would score high in virtually every contest he entered, and that his success in the competition would do much to restore the broken confidence and self-esteem of the Gurkoes. At length, Ganelon acquiesced, although he was still not happy with the idea.

The tribe which Ganelon and his friends had joined was called the Farz. The first contest was spear-throwing, and Silvermane hurled his spear so far it took an hour to find it.

He similarly outdistanced his fellow athletes by throwing the hammer and then the ax.

In the test of sword skills, later that afternoon, he held at bay five men considered agile with the rapier.

From the general melee, held just before nightfall, he emerged unscathed, the victor.

Only in chariot-racing and in the ornith-riding competition did his performance measure less than excellent. This was because of his very considerable weight, which slowed even the most powerful and spirited steed.

The winner of the Farz Tribe championship was judged to be Ganelon Silvermane.

Two or three days later his strength, agility, stamina and weapon skills enabled him to carry off the victory in a competition of the tribal winners for the Gurko Clan title.

Three days later he would compete with the other clans for the supreme championship of the entire Horde.

His former enemies now rallied around, vying one with the other to assist Ganelon Silvermane in successfully upholding the honor of the Gurko Clan before the full Horde assembled for the Greater Games.

Ganelon had fought in very different battles, on very different terrain, with very different weapons. His weapon of choice was the Silver Sword, that enchanted blade, forged by Fire Magic, and awarded him by the grateful Hegemons for his role in defeating the invasion of the Indigons.

But he had fought with the yarmak and the rapier, the scimitar and the pornoi. As well, Grrff had practiced him in fighting with sea-trident, ygdraxel, ax and war-hammer. Now the most skillful fighting men of the Gurkoes spent night and day teaching him how to fight with sting-sword, pike, dart-thrower and volusk. And Lord Barzik himself contributed to Ganelon's training by instructing him in the use of the giz. This was a jag-edged throwing-disc, razor-sharp and metallic.

Only Black Unggo and his henchman, Iquanux, failed to assist in the preparation of Silvermane. The surly lout and his toady bore heavy grudges against the young giant, and almost dared hope he would be brought down to ignominious defeat in the Greater Games.

The time drew near. Finally the day arrived.

In his tent, Ganelon lay on a couch, his muscles being massaged and pummeled into limberness by fat, black-bearded Larx, a subchief, while Harukh Irongrim and Lord Barzik imparted last-minute advice, counsel and warnings to their champion.

"Nothing we can do about the ornith races or the chariot competition, I fear," grumbled Lord Barzik worriedly. "The lad'll lose those events without question."

"He'll have to make up for losing those events by scoring extra points in the other competitions," said the dignified old chief, Irongrim, who had taken a fancy to the young giant. "The boy has a good chance to win with rapier, scimitar, yarmak and zikko."

"And he's a cinch to win the melee," added Wolf Turgo. "Not to mention the wrestling competition, and the boxing match."

Harsha smiled humorously. "*I* just wish he was as good at archery and throwing the giz as he is with ax, war-hammer and spear! Talk about piling up points—!"

"I have done all I can do to teach him the giz," declared Barzik frostily. "It is a skill you are either born with or you aren't. And he isn't, alas. In any competition based on speed, agility, or skill, the boy's in trouble. But in those where what really counts is stamina, strength, weight, endurance, or height, there's not a man in the entire Horde could best him."

"Save maybe Zaar," chuckled Harsha. The young Herald grinned even wider at the thought. "Gods, what a contest *that* would be—those two giants pitted together in man-to-man combat."

"A very unlikely event," smiled Wolf Turgo. "Ol' Warlord, he's not about to expose himself to the chance of being defeated. Not him."

Barzik and old Harukh Irongrim shifted their weight from one foot to another and cleared their throats uncomfortably. It did not do to speak lightly or slightingly of their brooding and enigmatic Master, whose savage temper and bloodthirsty ferocity, when roused, could be terrible. As soon as they could, they changed the subject.

The nine champions took the field at dawn before roaring thousands in a vast, oval-shaped arena east of Jurago.

In the first hour, Ganelon hurled the war-hammer farther

than it had ever been flung by human hands before, threw a longspear so far it vanished from sight, and hurled the ax to record distance.

In the second hour he lost the ornith race, the chariot, and the rope-dance competitions to, respectively, the Urzik, the Hoy, and the Kazool champions. But he was ahead on points, as none of these single-game champions managed to break an existing record, while Ganelon had broken all three in the first competition.

In the third hour he outwrestled and outboxed all nine Clan champions, flooring his opponents in record time, breaking the jaw of the Urzik and the clavicle of the Rooxa, and dislocating the right arm of the Tharrad.

In the fourth hour he lost the archery contest to the Kazool champion and the giz-throw to the Hoy athlete, and split first prize with the Fartha in the pornoi and in the dart-throwing games.

The fifth hour the champions rested, partook lightly of lunch, were sponged and pummeled by their masseurs, and listened to their coaches.

The sixth and seventh hours were devoted to the skills of the sword. While the Fartha and the Hoy champions were judged more skillful with longsword, rapier, and poignard than was Ganelon, his superior weight and strength, to say nothing of his enormous reach, made it possible for him to beat them to a draw.

On the other hand, he carried off the victory in contests with scimitar, broadsword, and sea-trident and came in second with the yarmak. He so powerfully fought with the broadsword that he lamed the Kazool and opened an artery in the arm of the Gurzi. These champions withdrew.

Later that afternoon he lost the contest in mounted archery to the Fartha, and mounted swordsmanship to the Hoy, and beat all contestants in roping and throwing a bull nguamadon.

The ygdraxel competition was canceled, since it was obvious that Ganelon had an unfair advantage over the other contestants, having been tutored by a genuine Tigerman.

Then it was dinnertime. The exhausted competitors limped or staggered off to their tents to soak in hot baths and eat and sleep.

On the second day of the Games, it was Silvermane who beat all other champions in the running and jumping and general endurance trials. Especially in those which required of the victor incredible stamina.

While the limber, long-legged Fartha champion easily ran faster than Ganelon, Ganelon beat everyone else in the mile run. And he won a thunderous ovation from the audience when he challenged all contestants to a twenty-mile race.* None of them was foolish enough to accept his offer, of course.

Later that day, the Fartha champion beat him in the high-jump, while Ganelon carried off the victory in the broad-jump, establishing a new record. In attempting to beat the mark set by Silvermane, the Fartha champion sprained his ankle and withdrew from the Games.

On the third and last day of the Games, it was Ganelon Silvermane who carried off the prize in test after test. He held up to eight opponents at bay with his sword, wrestled a captured Indigon to earth in two minutes, and broke the back of a cave-bear.

Then began the melee. This was the event for which the Ximchaks had been looking forward with the heartiest interest, for the melee was a pitched battle between opposing sides, like a miniature war. Ganelon was the Warchief of one side, the Purples, while the Hoy champion led the opposing side, called the Mauves.

Besides the champions themselves (or those who had survived thus far unscathed, at any rate), the two forces were composed of volunteers drawn from the more eager, blood-thirsty, or bored Ximchak warriors in the several Clans. They were ineligible for the Grand Championship, of course, and partook of the fray merely for good, healthy exercise, a desire to win notice and recognition, and perhaps reputation.

The melee began at a trumpet signal from the Herald mounted in the Warlord's box.

Ganelon fortified a hillcrest position, and drew his men into a line guarding the mount. They were protected by inter-

---

* Ganelon Silvermane could run at a steady pace for about three days without resting. No human champion could match him in grueling endurance tests. He was stronger and tougher than any True Man who had ever lived.

locking shields. When the Mauves charged this shieldwall it opened, on prearranged signal, revealing parallel avenues. Through these swept the mounted archers of the Purple. In the first ten minutes of battle the Hoy chief was down with an arrow through his brisket.

The Gurzi champion, his second-in-command, replaced him at the head of the Mauves. His buglers blew the signal: the Mauve heavy cavalry swung in two wings, charged and scattered the Purple archers. Ganelon gave the signal and his pikemen stepped through the shieldwall and went for the Mauves.

Waving their pikes like pinwheels, they sprinted down the slope, panicking the orniths. These bucked, reared, unseated most of the cavalry. The Purple pikes fell upon the cavalrymen and dispatched them bloodily.

The Gurzi chief sent his infantry to the relief of the distressed cavalrymen.

Ganelon had been waiting for that, and signaled his archers. A rain of barbed death sprayed the Mauve infantry as they slowly plodded up the slope to where the cavalry was being slaughtered. Staggering before the shower of arrow shafts, the infantry broke, sought shelter, or crouched, holding their shields over their heads.

Ganelon signaled: his axmen, hammer-throwers, zikkomen and broadsworders left the shieldwall and charged down the slope.

The neatly drawn lines of battle now blurred, intermixed, became a struggling, shouting mob. Through the sea of men Ganelon surged like a breaching whale, waded up to where the Gurzi chief sat his mount, caught him by one leg, and threw him to the ground.

The Gurzi sprang to his feet, roaring, snatched out his sword, and fell upon Silvermane, hewing lustily. Ganelon caught the blows upon the silver Sword, turned them aside without apparent effort, and swung his own mighty brand. It snapped the Gurzi's blade in two, cut entirely through his leather-on-wicker shield, and knocked the big man down, measuring his length upon the trampled snow, nursing a wounded shoulder. The Gurzi could fight no more.

Ganelon lifted his head and looked around him. His heavy infantry was slowly traversing the battlefield, axes and hammers, zikkoes and broadswords rising and falling, as they hewed a red path through the crumbling Mauves.

Mauve units were peeling away to either side now, falling away to left and right. When it became known that their leader, the Gurzi champion, had fallen, the disengagement became a rout, then a frantic stampede.

The battle was judged; the victors were the Purple; and Ganelon had won the final contest.

The following day, before the massed thousands of the Horde, he was proclaimed the Champion of all the Ximchaks. A full chieftaincy in the Gurkoes was awarded him, and Zaar the Warlord affixed upon the brows of Silvermane, with his own hands, the nine-feather plume of the Grand Champion.

Zaar glowered down upon him broodingly.

Ganelon Silvermane had been a member of the Horde for only three months and ten days. In that brief time, only a hundred days, he had risen from a despised and taunted recruit to a full chieftain of his Clan, and Grand Champion of the Ximchaks. So swift and spectacular a rise in popularity seemed inexplicable to Zaar.

It seemed also . . . *dangerous.*

Zaar resolved to watch this Outlander recruit closely and carefully. And, if necessary, be rid of him.

One way or another.

But Ruzara, who had shared the royal box with Zaar throughout the Games, viewed Silvermane in quite another light.

In reaction to her own people's disgusting incompetence in the manly arts of war, the Amazon girl had developed a fascination for masculine prowess.

Zaar, of all the Ximchaks, had seemed to her the most superb specimen of fighting manhood. So she had permitted the Warlord to lazily play at courting her favors during the long months of the occupation of Gompland by the Horde.

But now she had found another favorite.

Ganelon had thrilled the impulsive, passionate girl to the depths of her being. Her innate femininity had responded eagerly, instinctively, to his strapping height, his splendid physique, and to his bravery, and prowess, and strength, and skill.

51

Staring down at him now, her heart beating like a triphammer, the girl feared that her infatuation was visible in her flushed cheeks, her dreamy eyes, her half-parted lips. But no one seemed to notice her agitation, least of all Silvermane.

That was something she would have to attend to, in time.

Book Two

THE WARLORD OF WORLD'S END

The Scene: The Gompish Regime; The Quinthian Plains; Jurago, Luzzuma and Mungda; the Pergode Pass.

New Characters: The Shaman Kishtu; Bargon the Kazooli; Tharg of Erkon, Ovvo, Ruzik, Tharrad; Ulfwyn, Dygoth, and the other Ximchak Warchiefs.

6.

A CHIEFTAIN FOR THE GURKOES

In the weeks following the Greater Games, Ganelon Silvermane found himself no longer the spat-upon, mocked workhorse of a former-enemy-turned-recruit. He was indeed the Toast of the Host, if you will, and innumerable were the seasoned campaigners and veteran warriors who vied for his company. The change in the regard of the Ximchaks for Silvermane was total.

It was also understandable. Born warriors, the men of the Horde respected strength and skill and courage above all, admired prowess beyond anything, and the more *macho* a man the more popular he was with his comrades.

By winning the Grand Championship, by displaying his skills and endurance, leadership and bravery, before the massed Ximchaks, Silvermane had won their respect and admiration at one stroke. To win their affection would take a little longer.

When it was announced by Barzik, the Warchief of the Gurkoes, that Ganelon's reward from his Clan would be a full chieftainship, the younger, less experienced, more hero-worshipping of the Barbarians flocked to join his tribe.

It should perhaps be mentioned here that chieftainship in

the Horde was, as it were, both a civil honor and a military title.

Generally speaking, a chieftain was the leader of a tribe, although sometimes a tribe had two or even three chieftains. Each of the Nine Clans was composed of several tribes, indeed, of many tribes, in the instance of the larger Clans. At the period of its prime strength, for example, the Gurkoes has been made up of slightly more than two hundred tribes; at the time of which I write, they consisted of only some eighty.

Originally, each tribe had been a huge family, sometimes numbering more than one hundred members. But this was in the old days, back when the Ximchaks had been wandering nomadic hunters in the remotest north, before the Great Ximchak Migration had been launched by Zaar's father, Xoden. Because of intermarriage, and the natural process of elimination through almost constant warfare, and also extensive recruitment from the outlaws, malcontents, mercenaries, and vagabonds encountered during their march through many lands, the original blood kinship which had knit a tribe together was almost nonexistent by now.

Today, a tribe was little more than a military unit, usually called a Hundred, and, therefore, usually composed of about one hundred warriors. Where in the old days the chieftaincy had been hereditary, today it was appointive, as often as not.

Since the Farz tribe in which Ganelon had been, as it were, adopted already had not one chieftain but two, Black Unggo and Wolf Turgo, Lord Barzik permitted Ganelon to form his own tribe, which was to be called the Kuzak, that is, "the best."

There were many Gurko warriors who wished to join the new tribe, and still more who wished to come over from the other Clans, the Fartha, the Urzik, the Hoy, the Kazool, the Rooxa, the Gurzi, the Tharrad and the Qarr.

Before anybody noticed it, some two hundred and fifty warriors had enlisted in the new Kuzak tribe. At that point, Lord Barzik called a halt and declared the new tribe filled to strength. Three hundred latecomers were turned away.

As it so happened, this made the new tribe the largest single component in what was left of the Gurko Clan, which lent Ganelon considerable authority and added considerable importance to his role in the Council of Chieftains. When

Black Unggo learned of this, he was disgruntled, and ventured to complain to Barzik and Harukh Irongrim.

They commiserated with him as best they could, but their hearts were not really in it.

"After all, one reason we accepted Silvermane and his two comrades, Grrff and the sphinx-woman, into the Gurkoes in the first place, rather than slaughtering them out of hand, was that we were severely under strength and urgently needed every recruit we could find," reasoned Barzik gently.

"Quite so," nodded Irongrim, preening his gray beard. "And, actually, things could hardly have worked out more to our liking. Because of his victory in the Greater Games, and the popularity Silvermane has earned thereby, two hundred and fifty new recruits have joined the Gurkoes. We are nowhere near having our lost thousands restored, of course, but we're much better off than we were before."

"I fear you shall have to live with it, Unggo," said Lord Barzik, dismissing him.

"Aye," growled Unggo surlily. But once back with his flunky, Iquanux, he gave fullest vent to his spleen, knocking the whimpering fellow about until he took refuge under a cot, cringing and sniveling.

Feeling a trifle better, Black Unggo got roaring drunk.

Unggo's dislike of Ganelon Silvermane stemmed originally from the fact that Silvermane had been in command of the forces of Trancore in those battles and engagements whose result had been Unggo's utter and ignominious defeat.

When warlike thousands are crushed by a mere handful, well . . . you can't reasonably expect the leader of those thousands to become exactly bosom friends with the head of the handful.

Unggo nursed his rage in secret: in Council he was surly and argumentative—his normal manner, after all, which aroused no curiosity among his peers—and generally voted dead opposite to anything Silvermane had an opinion on.

This, too, did not attract any particular notice.

But Kishtu, who seldom missed a trick, did not miss this one, either.

The gaunt and sour old fanatic was a tribal Gurko shaman. The Ximchak shamanate, formerly in virtual possession of the supreme authority, had been reduced to a position of negligible, almost superfluous, importance under the regime of Xoden and his giant son, Zaar.

It was only natural for those two tyrants to chip away at the power base of any authority remotely close to their own. The shamanate had been diminished to a purely advisory role under Xoden; under Zaar, it had declined further, and now occupied a position of little more than titular authority.

Kishtu, one of the few shamans left in the Horde, clung with fierce tenacity to the vestiges of his former power. He would do anything to place the shamanate in the ascendancy again.

Thus, he played politics, did Kishtu, pitting this chief against that, scheming to turn friendly rivals into livid foes, jockeying for any slightest increment of power he could add to augment his slender store.

He hated Zaar, yet he envied him; in a way, he admired him.

He hated Ganelon from sheer principle: Ganelon was an Outlander, and Kishtu hated all foreigners. He was a former enemy, and Kishtu despised all enemies, former or otherwise. He was a recruit, almost a turncoat, and Kishtu loathed and distrusted all recruits, whether turncoats or otherwise.

The fact of the matter was that Kishtu, being Kishtu, hated, despised, loathed and distrusted almost everybody.

Even other shamans.

His cold, keen, quick, clever eyes noticed the disgruntlement of Black Unggo. It did not take him very long to observe that whenever Ganelon voted yea on anything, Black Unggo voted nay—regardless of what was being voted upon. A few questions here and there, a bit of quiet eavesdropping, a smidgin of bribery in the right places, and Kishtu had the whole story.

Black Unggo hated Ganelon Silvermane because he was bigger and stronger and braver and smarter and more successful and more popular than Black Unggo was.

These were the sort of emotions that the shaman Kishtu understood almost by instinct.

Black Unggo hated and resented Ganelon's swift, seemingly effortless rise to power. He hated him enough to murder him.

Now, *that* was interesting: very interesting.

Kishtu filed the information away under Current Business.

He might have a use for Black Unggo in his future plans.

He might have a use for Ganelon, too.

For the time being, he resolved to wait. Waiting was what Kishtu was very good at: almost as good as he was at scheming.

Time passed: winter locked the Gompish Regime in an iron grip.

In these, the Last Days near the End of the World and in the Twilight of Time, Old Earth was cooler than it had been ages before, and its sun was cooler, too: golden, now, no longer the fierce yellow-white of its brilliant prime, verging toward orange, even towards red-orange. The furious nuclear furnace that was its fiery heart burned now less fiercely than in our day. Summers were shorter and cooler, winters were lengthier and colder.

That winter whereof I write was, however, the longest and the bitterest that Gompland could remember. Food was in scant supply, so the Ximchaks killed and cooked and ate some of their steeds, first the nguamadons,* then the orniths. This was not quite the pointless and short-sighted slaughter that it may seem. There was hardly any forage for the nguamadons or the orniths, and many of them would have died anyway.

The Ximchaks survived, all but two hundred. They were tough, hard men, and used to privations. They gritted their teeth, tightened their belts, ate what they could when they could, and when they couldn't, they went hungry.

There was a joke circulated through the Ximchak tents about how, if things got much worse, they could always eat the Gomps. There were plenty of Gomps around, and, if anything, they were a lot hungrier than the Ximchaks. When the Ximchaks had little, the Gomps got less than little. By midwinter even the fat, waddling Gompish males were gaunt and stringy. "I'd rather eat an ornith than a Gomp," the camp

---

* Nguamadons are fat, waddling lizards used as saddle beasts in these parts of Gondwane the Great. Useless in the sprint, they are best in the long haul.

joke ran, "they got more fat on their bones." "Shucks, you'd be doing 'em a favor," ran the rejoinder, "after all, they're gonna die of starvation, anyway."

At that point the Ximchaks chuckled. But it was grim humor at best, and at worst there was a lot to it.

For the Gomps died by the thousands that terrible winter.

During the first month of his chieftaincy of the Kuzaks, Ganelon trained and exercised his men, turning them into skilled, seasoned warriors, familiar with every weapon and every trick and tactic of warfare.

By the middle of the second month, no finer band of fighting comrades existed among the eighty tribes of the Gurko.

All this time, the Warlord Zaar had watched the progress of Ganelon Silvermane from afar, even as had Black Unggo and the shaman Kishtu. He wanted to be rid of the potential menace which Ganelon Silvermane represented, as did Unggo and Kishtu.

But he wanted it to be arranged in such a way that his part in the death of Silvermane would remain unknown. It would never do for it to be known or even suspected that the Warlord Zaar *feared* Ganelon Silvermane, or any other man.

Soon a reasonable opportunity presented itself.

Silvermane had been training his troops for nearly two months now, and they were tough and feisty, beginning to get just a little mean-tempered due to inaction. Soon, unless work was found for them to do, they would begin to go sour.

Zaar found work for them to do.

A late, laggard spring had come to Gompery. The thaws set in, and the land was vile with rotting snow, dirty water, the earth turning to mud. The passes through the ring of mountains surrounding the Gompish lands would be open by now, and the question of which route to take became of paramount importance.

For Zaar knew that he had to lead the Ximchaks out of this realm of starvation and death, or they would turn and rend him, and choose another leader.

What more natural, then, but that Zaar should dispatch war parties to investigate the conditions at each of the Nine Passes?

And what more natural but that one of these should be a

large party of lusty Kuzaks, led by none other than their famous chieftain, the Grand Ximchak Champion, Ganelon Silvermane?

For the Kuzaks, Zaar selected one of the more distant passes, the Pergode, which gave forth upon the prospect to the east. It was far off and hard to get to, and the going was not only difficult, it was dangerous.

Which made it perfect for the brilliant, swaggering Kuzaks, and for their magnificent leader, of whose daring and courage and indomitable strength they so loudly and so loyally boasted.

Of course, there was very little point in checking out conditions at the Pergode Pass, because it opened upon Xoroth the Fire Desert, which was, of a certainty, not going to be used by the Ximchaks.

But, anyway, so the orders read.

And so it came to pass that, just two months and two days after he had led the Purples to victory in the melee and become the Grand Champion of all the Ximchaks, Ganelon Silvermane rode out through the North Gate of Jurago at the head of a picked hundred of his Kuzaks.

And—if Zaar had his way—he would never come back.

7.

THE KUZAKS RIDE NORTH

North of Jurago, the stone road led across an empty plain, once you were beyond the fringe of farms and groves and orchards which had encircled, and fed, the capital.

Of course, that was before the Ximchaks went carousing down through them, indulging in their Barbarian pleasures of looting, burning, plundering, and ravishment.

After the Ximchaks first passed through the farmlands, little was left standing, and the hard, cruel winter had finished off what little had been left.

Beyond the ruined farms and leveled groves, the north road led across the vast Quinthian Plain, where once Gompish luxherders had herded their huge, lumbering herds of lux.

Your common or garden lux is a large, amiable, grass-eating creature raised as beef cattle by the Gomps. They would resemble our own cows more closely if they were not pinkish-purple, and did not have quite so many curling silvery horns.

After the hungry winter just past, there were few lux left living, although there were still plenty of luxherders. Now unemployed, most of these had emigrated to one or another of the Thirty Cities, or had taken to yurgup farming.

The Quinthian was an endless plain of raw earth, like a coagulated sea or a desert of mud. Here and there, heavy masses of dirty, rotten snow still encumbered the level land, decaying in trickles of black water. Although winter was scarcely gone, a bright, yellow-green fuzz clothed the wet mud: before long, the Quinthian would be hip-deep in lush grasses. And, as it was now luxless, the meadow grass would go untrimmed.

For five days and nights, Ganelon Silvermane led his troop north and east across the grasslands, until on the evening of the fifth day they came within view of Mungda, a walled Gompish city which controlled the east-west caravan traffic—when there had been east-west traffic, that is. Sacked by the Barbarians a year or two before, the city was still only partially repaired. With the Ximchak takeover, of course, such merchant expeditions as had made the Mungdites fat with wealth had shrunk to nothing, and so had the Mungdites. Penniless, dispirited, they puttered with city repairs, but lacked the heart to work very hard at it.

The troop spent the night in a Mungdite hostelry, within view of the small Ximchak garrison outpost, and rode forth with dawn on the east road, bound for Luzzuma and the Pergode Pass.

Entering the Yellow Hills, they found their way made increasingly more hazardous by barriers of unmelted snow. The snow, sheltered from the erosion of wind and sun by the precipitous hill ridges, still lay thick, blocking the road. Ganelon led his men around the hills, although this extended their journey by another full day, rather than wear out men and saddle beasts in trying to negotiate the snow-blocked way through the hill country.

Approaching Luzzuma the following afternoon, they found this city one the Ximchaks had not ground to ruin under their heel. The Horde, Ganelon realized, had taken a more or less direct route south upon entering the Gompish Regime at its northernmost extremity, and had largely confined their ravaging and pillaging to the cities unfortunate enough to lie directly in their path on the journey south to Jurago.

The gates of Luzzuma were of indigo-blue marble, carved in olden times into the likeness of twin dragons, squatting on their hind members, facing each other, grinning jaw to jaw, as if squaring off for a fight. Through this gate they rode under the warm red light of a westering sun.

The chief of the Luzzuma garrison, one Bargon the Kazooli, had recognized Ganelon Silvermane the moment the bright-haired young giant came into view, and went forth to meet him. Ganelon was surprised and pleased to discover the garrison chief to be none other than the Kazooli champion who had bested him in the rope-dance and in the archery contests, and whom he had soundly beaten with the broadsword, soundly enough, in fact, to lame the warrior.

Solemnly shaking hands with the Kazooli, Ganelon inquired after his injuries, and expressed his relief at learning that the Kazool Clan champion had entirely recovered from the effects of their duel. As for Bargon the Kazooli, he was a tall man, taller than most Ximchaks, who rather tended toward being bowlegged from a lifetime spent largely in the saddle, and lighter than Silvermane, lithe, limber, and long-legged, with the trim, symmetrical physique of an experienced athlete. Silvermane had admired his nimble skill at the rope-dance, his keen eye and steady hand with the bow, and had found him in general a sportsmanlike and scrupulously honorable opponent. He was a trifle surprised to find him stationed here, in such an out-of-the-way post, until Bargon, with a shamefaced grin, confessed that Iotha, tribal chieftain of the Kazoolies, had bestowed this assignment upon him by way of punishment; having lost to an Outlander, the ireful Iotha deemed his performance in the Greater Games to have reflected considerable disgrace and loss of face upon his tribe.

That night Bargon and his officers feasted the Kuzaks right royally. So many toasts were drunk that more than a few of the warriors in Ganelon's force staggered off to bed somewhat the worse for the heady green Kazooli beverage they had so liberally downed. In the morning, many of them suffered the Ximchak equivalent of a hangover, to the alleviation of which medical science had come no nearer to effecting a cure in the seven hundred million years between our own time and Silvermane's era, than it had in all the ages since first the primal Summerian or perhaps Akkadian genius perfected the art of fermentation.

And thus it was a surly, queasy-stomached and headachy troop which Ganelon led east out of Luzzuma the following day. All that morning they followed the stone-paved road which rose gradually through the foothills. By early afternoon they reached the summit of the Pergode Pass and discovered that the snows were gone and the passageway was clear and open to travelers—if, indeed, any travelers should wish to venture in this unpromising direction.

For the remainder of that day the Kuzak warriors scouted the pass and foothills which lay to either side of the mountain wall which formed the eastern borders of the Gompish realm. From the hills they enjoyed a clear vista of Xoroth the Fire Desert to the east. As far as the unaided eye could perceive there extended a parched land of dry hot sand and tumbled stone fragments, riven by steaming crevices and pocked, here and there, by fumaroles like high-walled craters. Resembling miniature volcanoes, these protuberances leaked ragged plumes of sulfurous smoke. Occasionally, a hot lake of bubbling reddish mud could be observed, from which, at uncertain intervals, geysers of superheated fluids shot thunderously into the air.

No living thing was to be seen in all this parched and unappetizing wasteland, nor was there any sign that man had ever inhabited this desert region, save, of course, for the raised stone causeways which traversed the waste. These had been erected by the Tensors of Pluron about half a million years before, and did not therefore qualify as tokens of human habitation, since no one has ever maintained, in light of the distinct and incontrovertible evidence to the contrary, that the Pluronese Tensors had been even remotely human, evolved, as they were, from a now-extinct race of coldly intelligent insects.

It was on the ride back to Luzzuma that the incident occurred.

The dusk was thickening around them when suddenly Ganelon gave voice to a choked cry and slumped forward in the saddle. In the next moment he slid to one side and fell to the ground.

Riding at his side at the time was Tharg of Tharrad, one of the nine Clan champions who had so admired his prowess in the Games as to volunteer for service under him. Tharg bellowed the alarm, that they were under attack from unseen ambushers, and leaped from the saddle to tend his fallen chief.

Grrff the Xombolian, who had been riding directly ahead of Ganelon, had glimpsed the momentary twinkle of sunlight glancing from the polished wood of an arrowshaft, as the hurtling missile briefly bisected a level and ruddy beam cast by the sinking sun. His keen catlike eyes noted the source from which the shaft had presumably originated: roaring in outrage and challenge, the Tigerman pulled his steed about and flew into the shadows on thundering hooves,* intent upon the cowardly assassin.

The arrow had been shot from the crest of the nearest hill, a steep-sided prominence whose slope was too sheer for even an ornith to scale. Reining up, Grrff crouched in the saddle and sprang like the enraged tiger he so closely resembled. His extended claws raked the rocky ledge at the hillcrest—slid—screeching—then clung.

In an instant the sinewy Tigerman had gained the crest. The light was dim, but he could make out three muffled figures scurrying down the far slope toward saddled orniths. About to take up the pursuit, he stumbled over an unseen obstacle, and looked down to ascertain it.

It was a bow, with a quiver of arrows.

A *gompish* bow.

Action, not thought, was Grrff's way. His instinct was to fling himself upon these despicable assassins who had so cowardly struck down his friend and comrade from ambush. But he was afoot, and on the hilltop, while they had already gained their mounts and, even at that moment, were heaving themselves into the saddle.

There was no chance he could reach them before they left the scene of their crime as swiftly as the quick-footed orniths could carry them.

Without a moment's hesitation, without conscious thought, the Tigerman lifted the bow he still held, fitted an arrow into place, and let it fly. One of the assassins screeched, cursed,

---

* Clittering claws, actually, as Grrff was mounted upon an ornith, and they have long, strong, beclawed feet resembling those of the long-extinct ostrich.

clutched his arm. In the next instant the three rode out of the defile and vanished around the curve of the next hill base. Stagnant purple shadows drowned the light at that level, and further view was impossible.

Grrff descended the hill, clutching the assassin's bow, and bellowed until he attracted the alert ear of the nearer Kuzaks. He directed them to pursue the assassins, three in number, ornith-mounted, muffled in dark hooded cloaks, heading that-away.

They galloped off, faces set in grim, vengeful expressions.

He returned to where Silvermane lay, tended by Tharg and the others. At his approach, the Tharradian raised a scowling, worried face and a red-tipped arrow.

They had without difficulty extracted the shaft, which had been slowed by the heavy jerkin of black leather Ganelon had worn covering his chest. Removing the arrowhead from Ganelon's heart had also proved easier than they might have feared. Such was the superhuman density of the Construct's flesh that the barbed tip of the arrow had scarcely been able to penetrate his skin by more than a fraction of an inch.

Had the bow been aimed by a stronger arm, or had Ganelon's flesh been as tender as that of a True Man, the shaft would undoubtedly have transfixed his heart, killing him instantly. As it was, it had hardly more than pricked his skin.

That prick, however, might prove as fatal to Silvermane as if the arrow had indeed gone to the heart.

For the arrowhead was wet with a vile greenish liquor.
Poison.

Although the wound was slight, obviously the poison was extremely virulent and had already entered the veins of Ganelon Silvermane, for the young giant had already lapsed into unconsciousness, his features unnaturally pale with a sickly hue, and his torso, bared when they had stripped the leather jerkin away to remove the arrow, wet with cold, unhealthy perspiration, despite the bitter chill of the evening.

They could do little for him here, so, rigging a hammock-like stretcher, which they suspended from between the saddlehorns of two orniths riding side by side, they bundled Silvermane therein, wrapped him to the chin with blankets, and rode with all speed for Luzzuma.

They neither bandaged his wound nor sought to staunch the flow of blood. If he was poisoned, as seemed obvious, the more freely he bled, the less poison would enter his system.

Grrff stayed behind, waiting for the patrol to return from chasing the assassins. To kill the time, he searched the narrow-walled defile wherein the ambushers had tethered their orniths.

He found nothing of particular interest, but he did find the Gompish arrow he had sent after the fleeing three. It had indeed hit at least one of them, though only with a grazing shot. This he knew because there was blood on the shaft, but none on the arrowhead.

He recalled the guttural, choked cry one of the assassins had voiced, and how he had bent over, nursing one arm.

The *left* arm.

It was interesting ... also, it was a pity, he thought, that it had not been the poisoned arrowhead that had struck the Gomp in the arm. Had it been so, at least one of the three assassins would be dying right now, writhing in horrible agony, suffering even as Ganelon Silvermane was suffering.

Grrff grinned wickedly, thinking of the poisoned Gomp, baring his fangs. A pity he had not loosed the arrow truer to the mark: ah, well, the ygdraxel was more his weapon. And he had been overeager in firing off the arrow.

The squad returned, glum-faced, having lost the three Gomps somewhere in the darkness.

They rode back to Luzzuma gloomily, saying nothing because there was nothing to say.

8.

BARGON THE KAZOOLI DEDUCES

When Bargon learned of the assassination attempt upon the life of the Grand Champion, he was as livid with fury as one of his chocolate-skinned race can be.

At his command, squadrons combed the Quinthian Plains far and wide, searching for a party of Gomps. Fast riders rode at breakneck speed for the next nearest city, Mungda, to alert the garrison there against a possible Gomp uprising, and commanding them to close the east-west road, and the north-south road, against any and all traffic, warning them to be on the lookout for a party of three.

They found nothing, which was not surprising. There were ten thousand places where such a small force of men could conceal themselves, on the endless plains.

Silvermane had fallen into a deep coma by now. His heartbeat was erratic, his breathing shallow and labored. He was evidently in considerable pain. Her could keep no food down and his fever was rising steeply.

The Ximchaks knew little of the medical arts, but did what little they could. Grrff bade Bargon let Gompish physicians tend the stricken champion. The Tharradian looked shocked: had it not been Gomps who had ambushed him in the first place? How could they reasonably trust Gompish mediciners not to smother or poison yet further their charge?

Grrff bristled, then shrugged.

"The big man's near dead as it is," he growled. "Keep an eye on the Gomps while they fuss with him, and gut the first one that looks crosseyed or does anythin' suspicious. Besides, ol' Grrff ain't all that sure it wuz a Gomp what loosed that arrow."

"Why d'you think that?" demanded Bargon the Kazooli.

Grrff let his hooked claws go *snikk* in and out.

"Well, the *bow* was Gompish; so wuz th' arrow," he rumbled meaningfully. "But the hand what loosed it coulda been Ximchak, easy as Gomp."

"You got a point there," Bargon said thoughtfully, rubbing one big hand over a stubbled jaw. "Warko, go fetch the best Gomp doctors left in Luzzuma. *Jump!*"

By midnight seven very nervous and uncomfortable Gompish physicians were attending the unconscious Silvermane. They were applying cold packs in an attempt to reduce his raging fever, without, however, noticeable results. His half-closed wound they reopened, and they poulticed the raw cut with strong, poison-absorbing herbs. Guards stood about, watching them with hard, suspicious eyes, drawn swords at the ready.

Bargon had promised to feed the guard's ears to the yerxels if they let the Gomps dispatch Silvermane unnoticed.

The Gomps, however, did nothing even slightly suspicion-making, and labored all night to save the dying superman.

The messengers returned from Mungda with word that no party of three had entered the city, and that no travelers had approached the city at all.

They in Mungda also reported compliance with Bargon's command that all roads be closed until further notice.

As for the feared Gompish uprising, it did not materialize.

By dawn, Ganelon was still in a coma, and his fever was still unbroken.

However, he was still alive, and that was something.

The Gompish physicians, having been unable to do more than merely to stabilize Ganelon's condition, withdrew.

The chieftain was guarded around the clock by his Kuzaks. It was all they could do for him now, and they did it with vigilance and devotion.

There was still hope. The vigor and strength and stamina of Ganelon Silvermane were far greater than that ever recorded of a human being. While the name and nature of the poison remained unknown, it was at least conceivable that his magnificent body might yet throw off the effects of the venom of its own accord.

The Ximchaks had many gods, but little belief in them. Nevertheless, they prayed, each in his own way.

So did Grrff the Xombolian. Galendil the Good (he reasoned) had permitted the Time Gods to build the synthetic superman for a purpose yet unknown. Surely, Galendil would not permit him to die before fulfilling the destiny for which he had been created.

He wished Ganelon's mentor, the Illusionist of Nerelon, were there.

He wished Palensus Choy or Ollub Vetch were there, too.

He wished *somebody* was there! It was agony for him to sit by Ganelon's deathbed all alone, with no one else to share the dreadful burden.

The day passed, slowly.

Night fell. Ganelon's energies seemed to wane. Along toward the third hour after midnight, when, reputedly, the tides of life ebb to their lowest and death most frequently comes, the heartbeat of Silvermane grew faint. His breathing was scarcely audible; barely could you discern the rise and fall of his mighty chest.

Grrff ground his teeth and twisted his paws together until they went numb. The terror of it was, quite simply, that there was *nothing he could do to help.*

The bell struck four in the morning.

Ganelon's heart stopped beating.

Grrff let the hot salt tears gush from his eyes, wetting his furry cheeks. He threw back his head and from the depths of his being there wailed forth an animal-like, ululating cry.

The guards around the bed cursed and groaned, faces twisting in the ugliness of a man's grief.

Then something happened. . . .

About seven months before this, while a prisoner in Shai in the Land of Red Magic, Ganelon Silvermane had suffered a mind probe at the hands of a Ningevite Mentalist named Varesco. In probing deeply beneath the levels of consciousness and the centers of instinct, this Varesco was surprised to discover the existence of nine centers previously unmapped by the Mentalists of Ning. He had no idea of their nature or purpose, nor of the strange powers and abilities they controlled, but they seemed dormant and still unused.

He would have explored them further, but just then the boy Phadia had driven a steel needle through his brain and Varesco abruptly, and permanently, lost interest.

In the very instant that Silvermane's heart ceased all activity, one of these dormant mind centers—*awoke*.

A stream of thought-impulses surged through the nerve channels of the dying giant; a system of glands, also previously unknown to the mediciners of Gondwane, received their long-awaited stimulus.

They discharged an unidentifiable fluid into the bloodstream of Ganelon Silvermane.

Suddenly, his sickly pallor vanished. He flushed crimson. Perspiration burst from every pore in his skin. Unlike the greasy sweating occasioned by his fever, this particular exudation was curiously granular in nature, and tinged distinctly greenish.

The sweat rolled down his hide. He continued to sweat. Now his heartbeat stirred sluggishly, faltered into life again.

Grrff opened his eyes and saw what was happening. He did not understand what was happening, of course, but he suspected that—somehow—the body of Ganelon Silvermane was throwing off the effects of the poison.

Noticing the peculiar greenishness of the beads of perspiration rolling down the chest of Silvermane, Grrff damped one paw in the stuff, lifted it to his nostrils, and sniffed.

He recognized the odd citrus-sharp smell of the green poison. And he raised his voice in a roar, commanding basins of hot water and clean, dry cloths. He put the shaken, unbelieving guards busily to work sponging the green exudation from Silvermane's naked body.

One of the mysterious mind centers within Silvermane, obviously, was designed to help him resist the effects of poison.

It had triggered the glandular system into producing a cata-
lyst which broke down, neutralized, and flushed out of his
body the residue of the poison.

By midmorn Silvermane had stopped sweating, having rid
his system of the last traces of the venom.

His color regained its natural hue. His heartbeat was no
longer erratic, but pulsed strongly at an ordinary rate. His
breathing was deep and strong, normal, his temperature that
of a healthy man.

His fever vanished. So did the deep coma. He fell into a
calm, refreshing sleep, from which he awoke the next morning, weak as a jerbit, but well on the way to mending.

Grrff, Tharg and Bargon celebrated that evening in the
garrison's command post, by downing more wine than two
Ximchaks and a Tigerman ought to have been able to drink.
They became splendidly, roaringly, delightedly drunk.

"Sure glad Kurdi stayed behind," burbled the Xombolian
woozily. "Cub woulda worried hisseff sick over th' big man.
Damn them tricksy Gomps, or whoever they wuz did 'm
dirty."

"Not Gomps, nossir," said Bargon, shaking his shaggy head
definitely.

"Howcum you say 'not Gomps'?" demanded Tharg of
Tharrad sleepily. "Sure wuzza Gompy arrow . . ."

"Howcum I say not Gomps?" Bargon the Kazooli inquired
rhetorically. "Tell ya howcum I say not Gomps. *Why* 'ud
Gomps wanna bump off th' big fella? They ain't fonda
Ximchaks, sure: we mowed 'um up and mopped 'um down.
Hmm. Mowed 'um down, and mopped 'um up, I mean. But
big fella, he ain't no Ximchak. They got nuffin agin' *him*."

"Gotta point there, Bargon," rumbled Grrff thoughtfully.

"Dang right!" nodded the Kazooli. "Now, ol' Gomp, he
wanna git us riled or sumthin', *hurt* us, y'know, he gonna
knock off a Clan Warchief, one o' th' *big* brass. He ain't
gonna fool around bumpin' off no *tribe* chief like Ganelon.
Nossir! Hunnerds o' them around, they ain't that important.
Know what I mean?"

"Gotcha," mumbled Tharg. "Gomps wanna do us harm,
they gonna go after ol' Zaar hisseff, or Barzik, or Erkon, or
Ovvo Redtooth, or . . ."

"Right!" hiccuped Bargon. "So, mebbe hit were a *Ximchak* what done hit . . . some bum what don' like big fella, jealous a him, hates him, like—"

"Like Black Unggo," said Grrff, suddenly cold sober.

"Like Black Unggo, sure," nodded Bargon. "Or his crony, thet whimperin' pig-face, Iquanux—"

"Or ol' pizzen-face, *you* know, Kishtu," grunted Tharg.

Unggo.

Iquanux.

And Kishtu.

That made *three* prime suspects.

And Grrff had seen *three assassins* fleeing from the scene of their crime!

Suddenly, the furry Karjixian came lurching to his feet, nearly knocking over the table.

"Where y' goin', Grrff? Night's young and we still got us a dozen more bottles," protested Bargon the Kazooli.

"Gotta get some sleep," rumbled the Tigerman ominously. "Ol' Grrff's gotta get up early t'morra. Gonna take th' big man back t' Jurago."

"Whuffor?"

A red glint the color of murder gleamed in the eyes of Grrff the Xombolian.

"Wanna find out if Unggo and Iquanux and Kishtu been away recently," he said purringly. "And wanna see if one o' them three got hisseff a *scratch* on 'is left arm."

"Oh, ho," snorted Bargon, nodding wisely.

"An' if'n he does, ol' Grrff's gonna have his guts fer lunch, or die tryin'," said Grrff the Xombolian, leaving the room.

Despite Grrff's wishes, it was a week before Ganelon was well enough to travel, and even then the journey south had to be made in slow and easy stages with frequent rest stops.

It had taken the Kuzak troop six days to reach Luzzuma. It took them ten days to make the return trip. On the noontide of the twelfth day they rode back through the north gate of Jurago, and Silvermane by this time had sufficiently recovered his strength to be in the saddle. He had lost a little weight, and there were lines in his face that had not been there before, and he used his left arm a bit gingerly, but otherwise he seemed to be pretty much his own self.

Unggo, seeing the giant in the saddle, waving to the cheering Ximchaks who still remembered with admiring awe his prowess in the Greater Games, gulped, swallowed painfully and turned the unhealthy color of muddy milk.

Zaar glowered with thunderous brow, and turned a fierce glare upon the hulking, astounded bully that would have withered an ooga-ooga tree in its tracks. Unggo swayed, eyes popping.

And the sharp eyes of Grrff saw it all.

And marked Black Unggo down for death.

9.

THE TELLTALE SCAR

Ganelon and his Kuzaks returned to their camp, and in no time the word of the ambush and of the attempted assassination of the Grand Champion of the Horde spread throughout the Ximchak army. Anger and outrage were expressed, and more than a few of the Barbarians swore vengeance upon the cowardly assassins, should ever their names or identities be discovered.

Such was the esteem in which Ganelon Silvermane was held by his adopted brethren. And, as his Kuzak warriors told the full account of his amazing recovery from the wound above the heart and the unknown poison, a curious degree of reverence now came to augment the hero-worship which shone about him. His recovery was deemed miraculous, and further demonstrated the theory, held by some, that he was the chosen instrument and darling of the gods.

This last theory had been spreading through the Nine Clans during the last six months, or ever since Silvermane had joined the Gurkoes. Its beginnings were in the brilliant succession of victories Silvermane had enjoyed when he had fought against the Horde at Valardus, Mount Naroob, Trancore and the Ovarva Plains. Since he had voluntarily become

76

a Ximchak, it was theorized that his remarkable luck—if that was all it was—would now be on the side of the Ximchaks.

His swift, unerring rise to popularity, his glorious triumph in the Games, and now the miracle of his recovery from the nameless poison, all went to further support the belief, by now quite widespread, that Ganelon Silvermane was under the direct, personal protection of some god.

The Ximchaks, as noted earlier, had little faith in their own tribal divinities. Yet, like all savages, they were hopelessly superstitious. It followed naturally, therefore, that in their estimation power resided in the gods worshipped by others: in this case, by the god worshipped by Ganelon Silvermane, who was none other than Galendil the Good.

The cult of Galendil increased the number of its followers quite rapidly among the Hordesmen.

For some two weeks after his return to Jurago, Silvermane rested, exercised, ate hugely, slept frequently, and concerned himself essentially with the complete restoration of his powers.

By the end of the second week, he had not only completely recovered from his narrow brush with death, but was in finer form than he had been in years. Not since his enlistment in the Zermish militia, and the battle against the marauding herds of Indigons that had come down from the north to imperil the Hegemonic cities, had he been in such superb condition. His strength was greater even than before, his stamina and endurance superior to any he had previously enjoyed, and he was spoiling for a showdown with his would-be assassins.

For in the interim between his return to Jurago and now, Grrff the Xombolian and Tharg of Tharrad, his chief lieutenants, had been busy.

Adroit and carefully casual questions, placed in the proper quarters, and oiled with a bit of flattery and a little bribery, had elicited the information that at the same time Ganelon Silvermane had been absent from the capital on his expedition to the Pergode Pass, two other members of the Horde had inexplicably been absent, as well.

These two were none other than Black Unggo and his henchman, Iquanux. As for the shaman Kishtu, no one could quite recall whether he had been around or not.

The explanation of Unggo's absence was given out as a hunting expedition. However, it had been noticed by more than a few that when the chieftain had at length, and hastily, and in a suspiciously surreptitious manner, returned to Jurago, he had with him no carcasses of game.

Either the hunting had gone badly, or perchance Unggo had really been after another kind of game. . . .

Grrff the Xombolian thought he knew the answer. The game Unggo had hunted went on two legs, had long silvery hair, and went under the name of Ganelon.

Ganelon, however, was not entirely certain. His simple and trusting nature was such that he found it difficult to believe in the iniquity of men like Unggo and Iquanux. In many ways as innocent as a child, he tended to take men at their face value, and would only believe them to be traitors when proofs of their treachery were incontrovertible.

On the very next day the Warlord had summoned the Great Council to a meeting in the Barzoolian Palace. The Great Council differed from the Council of the Clans in that all of the chieftains of the tribes, as well as the Warchiefs of the Nine Clans, were met together to discuss pressing affairs.

In the vast hall, cushions had been laid out in long rows to accommodate the chieftains in their hundreds. Among these were Ganelon Silvermane, attended by Grrff and little Kurdi, Harsha of the Horn, and Black Unggo, attended by his subchief, Iquanux.

Also present were Lord Barzik and Harukh Irongrim, the Gurko leaders, and the Warchiefs of the other Clans, among them Erkon of the Hoy, Ovvo Redtooth of the Fartha, and Arnhelm Blackshield of the Kazool Clans.

Zaar was seated in his great throne, a somber, brooding giant in black iron and black leather, with Kishtu the shaman at his side.

Zaar, it seemed, had been unable to select an avenue of withdrawal from Gompland that did not smack of retreat. Neither had the Council of the Clans arrived at a decision on this matter, each Warchief holding views directly contradictory to each other. It was hoped that, from this convening of all the tribal chieftains, a clear consensus might emerge.

For some time the proposals and arguments and counterproposals droned on, as each man sought his chance to have his say, whether or not he had anything to say, merely in order to enhance his own importance.

Then, quite suddenly, there occurred a small diversion which was to have the most dramatic consequences, and was to influence the destiny of many nations for the duration of man's habitation on Old Earth.

Sometimes events of vast and momentous impact hinge upon the slightest, most trivial of accidents. Dramatists have always realized this basic truth by pure instinct, whereas most historians tend to overlook the accidental and trivial in favor of the interaction of vast political or economic forces.

In this particular case, however, it was the trivial that changed history—the mere slipping down of a leathern cuff.

Wine was being served to the chieftains, as much to loosen their wits as to moisten throats dry with speechifying. Eager for his, Black Unggo did not wait for the Gompish servitor to place the goblet before him, but reached up to take it.

He soon had cause to regret his thirstiness.

Unggo wore, it seems, upon his left forearm, a leathern cuff or broad strap. No one, afterward, could recall having seen him affect this ornament previously. In reaching up, the play of his muscles must have loosened its grip upon his beefy arm, for, in lowering the cup to drink, the cuff slid down to his wrist.

Exposing a certain scar.

Grrff sprang to his feet, roaring. The feisty Tigerman had dreamed of this moment: for days and days he had sought a look at the left forearm of Black Unggo, to see if there was upon that arm a scratch or scar, of recent vintage, such as could well have been made by the glancing blow of an arrowshaft. And there it was!

With a deep, coughing growl of challenge, Grrff fixed the loutish chieftain with a glaring eye. Whiskers bristling, hackles up, claws out, he leaped across the aisle of squatting chiefs to pounce upon his prey like the great tawny cat he was.

Seizing the astounded and speechless Unggo by the scruff of the neck, the Tigerman dragged him to his feet, tore off the leather band with a single slash of his razory claws, and displayed the offending limb before all eyes. There was a raw red cut, newly healed.

"What is the meaning of this outrage?" thundered Zaar, rising to his feet and glowering down upon the Xombolian.

"This wound wuz made by ol' Grrff, shooting an arrow after the danged assassin what tried to murder the big man over there from ambush," growled Grrff.

"It ain't true . . . I weren't there . . . I wuz huntin'," blustered Unggo, striving to wriggle free of the Karjixian Tigerman's grip.

"You cannot assault a full chieftain in Council convened," said Zaar in a voice as cold and hard and heavy as iron. "Release that man, return to your camp, and place yourself under arrest."

"Ol' Grrff can challenge this black dog to single combat, though, can't he?" argued the Tigerman, who had been careful to ascertain the Horde law upon personal challenges to combat.

Zaar opened his mouth to make some answer, but whatever he intended to say, it was never said. For Lord Barzik spoke up first.

Fixing the flushed, angry, apprehensive Unggo with a cold, measuring eye, the Warchief said in a clear, ringing voice:

"By Horde law, any chieftain may challenge any other chieftain to personal combat during this Council."

"I—" began Zaar.

"By Horde law, during this Council, all present are considered to be of equal rank, and the lowliest subchief is thereby equivalent to the Warlord himself," spoke up Ovvo Redtooth.

"Aye, were it not so, the vote of a Clan Warchief would not be equal to the vote of tribe chieftain or subchief, and vote-countin' would be meaningless," nodded Erkon of the Hoys.

"And if yonder black-avised dog tried to murder the lad— the Grand Champion, I mean!—from ambush, I'll challenge the cowardly pig myself, once yonder catman is through with him, if there's anything left by that time, that is," swore Dygoth of the Rooxa Clan.

The other Warchiefs eyed Unggo ominously, contemptuously, and levelly. The hulking Unggo, a bully at heart but a coward to the roots of his soul, licked his lips, measured the towering, furry, muscular height of the grinning Tigerman with eyes suddenly fearful, and began to whine and blubber. The very sight of those sharp, terrible claws, like grisly iron hooks, struck him livid with terror. He cast a gaze, frightened and imploring, at Zaar.

Zaar wavered a fraction of a second, then sat back and turned an expressionless gaze upon Grrff.

"Very well," he said harshly. "The challenge is lawful, and cannot be refused. Name the time and the place."

"Here," growled the Karjixian, baring white fangs in a leering grin. "And now."

Zaar frowned. "You would delay the serious business of this Council with your personal quarrel?"

Grrff exposed his black claws, grinning.

"Once ol' Grrff gets these into the fat guts o' this black dog," said Grrff, "he'll make those blubber-lips sing a tune o' truth. And all the chiefs of the Horde'll hear from Unggo's mouth who rode with him to the Yellow Hills that day—for there were *three men* who lurked in ambush for the big man t' go ridin' by!"

Iquanux turned the color of sour milk, gulped, and wet suddenly dry lips. And Kishtu, beside the throne, sank back into the shadows with a sly, slinking movement, like a startled viper recoiling. And many there were in the hall who saw and noted their reactions to the Tigerman's words.

"By Horde law, the challenger has the right to name the place and the hour of the combat, and none may say him nay," growled old Ulfwyn of the Gurzimen. "Let the lad have his will, Lord."

"Aye, let 'em fight it out, and mayhap we'll wring the truth from this Gurko assassin," said Ruzik of the Tharradians.

Zaar started to speak, thought better of it, and subsided, his expression grim.

"Clear space and let the battle commence," he bade the servants.

In a trice the low tabourets and cushions were cleared away, opening a circular area about thirty feet across. Kurdi ran to fetch Grrff his Karjixian ygdraxel while Iquanux scurried out to bring Black Unggo's battleax.

And the fight began.

It was soon over. A bully growls and swaggers only so long as no man dares to call his bluff. Once called, however, it soon becomes apparent that he has nothing in him but bluff.

Unggo threw himself at Grrff with a fury born of utter desperation. For a brief while, his beefy weight and berserker tactics kept the Xombolian on the defensive. But not for long. Grrff was an experienced warrior, and a veteran of rough-and-tumble, and knew how to bide his time. He held himself back, permitting Unggo to wear himself out. Before very long, the loutish subchief was scarlet-faced and puffing like a beached whale.

Then the Tigerman pressed the attack, beating the bully back with deft, dazzling strokes of his ygdraxel. Within minutes, Unggo was staggering blindly, streaming blood from a dozen small, inconsequential wounds, his defenses crumbling.

One slashing, twisting dart of the ygdraxel and its keen metal claws closed over the handle of the war ax, snatching it from Unggo's enfeebled grasp. Then Grrff lunged forward and took him by the throat. Eyes filled with pure animal terror, the Gurko goggled fearfully up into the Tigerman's burning gaze.

"Speak, dog, or die!" growled Grrff, shaking him by the throat as a terrier shakes a rat. "It was you tried to scrag the big man, wasn't it?"

"Y-yes! Don't kill poor Unggo! *Don't!*" babbled that worthy, hugging the Tigerman's knees. " 'Twas Unggo, aye—*but Zaar made me do it. . . .*"

The room became utterly still. In a silence so deafening you could hear the blood ringing in your ears, the Warlord came slowly, stiffly to his feet, his brow black and thunderous.

No one dared speak or stir. No one dared even look at him as he stood there, clenching and unclenching his great scarred fists.

Grrff gave Unggo one last shake, then cast him from him. Unggo huddled blubbering, face down on the pave. Grrff spat, and turned away.

Silvermane came slowly to his feet, his face as hard and as bleak as it had been a deathmask cast in cold bronze.

In the ringing silence, his voice was like an iron bell, tolling doom.

"By the law of the Horde, I hereby challenge the Warlord Zaar to personal combat," he said expressionlessly.

Then, borrowing a leaf from Grrff's book, he added:

"Here, and now."

10.

DUEL OF THE TITANS

Excitement and anticipation ran high. The Warchiefs, chieftains, and subchiefs of the Nine Clans could not recall within recent memory such a portentous occasion, or a more dramatic confrontation than that which impended.

None of them had ever thought it likely that a champion should arise within the Horde powerful and brave enough to challenge the mighty Zaar to ritual combat. And, indeed, for any lesser mortal than Ganelon Silvermane to have done so would have been accounted folly by them all.

There were those who regarded the duel in a dubious manner. After all, Zaar was one of their own, while Silvermane was only a newcomer, a recent recruit, a stranger to their ranks. But even these would have conceded their disapproval and dissatisfaction of Zaar; in the past year or two, his decisions had been generally disastrous for the Horde. He had first led the Ximchaks into the cul-de-sac of Gompery, and then had been unable to find a way out.

Perhaps it was time for a change. This Silvermane was certainly a redoubtable warrior, a born leader, a true champion of champions. He had been among them less than seven months withal, but even within so brief a span of time he had won the respect, the admiration and the esteem of most of the Horde's leaders. In dramatic contrast to Zaar, everything he had attempted he had accomplished, and his every act had been crowned with victory.

And, if it were actually true that Zaar had secretly conspired with Unggo to murder from cowardly ambush the popular new champion, then in the opinion of the majority of the Ximchak leadership, he deserved death.

Many remembered that Zaar had achieved the Warlord's rank not through the time-honored process of trial-by-challenge and defeat of the former Warlord, but by election and fiat of the former Warlord. If Silvermane succeeded in dislodging him from the summit, it would be a return to the original Ximchak tradition, and therefore welcome.

So the leaders settled back with curiosity, eagerness, and a certain trepidation, to await the outcome of the contest.

No matter how it might turn out, the battle would certainly afford them a spectacle such as none of them had ever witnessed before—truly, a battle royal between giants!

The two were to fight barehanded, there in the center of the vast hall. The Horde law forbade the use of an enchanted weapon in a contest for the supreme office, and Silvermane disdained the employment of any lesser weapon.

Stripped and in readiness for the battle, the two presented a magnificent example of fighting manhood. They were evenly matched in height and weight and in muscular development, and both contestents were grimly aware that from this duel, only one survivor would emerge.

Harsha sounded his horn and the two giants began circling each other, warily, tossing punches lightly, feeling out the other's guard.

Then they closed, grappling, launching hammerlike blows which thudded with meaty smacks. Any one of those blows landing upon an ordinary man would have hospitalized him for a week or more, but the two gladiators hardly seemed to feel their impact.

Ganelon drove a powerful left that staggered Zaar. Swiftly recovering, the Warlord countered with a hammering right that dazed the silver-haired giant. Again they closed, fists flailing, pounding away at each other.

In no time both men were running with blood from small wounds, their bodies slick and gleaming with sweat. The chieftains watched in fascinated silence.

Thunk! A trip-hammer right to the gut folded Silvermane and left him gasping. He struck out with an uppercut which connected with Zaar's jaw and sent him crashing back against a chair, which shattered beneath his weight. Kishtu helped him to his feet, murmuring something in his ear.

The Warlord nodded dazedly—or was he merely shaking his head to clear his wits?—and lunged at Silvermane again, smashing powerful blows to his chest and belly.

Now it was Ganelon's turn to stagger back, folding under the rain of blows. Never before had he endured such terrific punishment! Never before, save perhaps in battle with the Indigons, had Ganelon fought an opponent as large and strong and powerful as Zaar. The power of his smashing blows was terrific, Ganelon staggered, reeling beneath the impact of those great fists. Each blow to his body was like being hit with a sledgehammer, and had he not been Ganelon Silvermane, it is doubtful that he could have endured as long as he had the punishment his body was absorbing. He fell to his knees.

Somehow he got to his feet again, shrugging off the hammering fists, and struck back with all his strength, in the sure knowledge that if he did not win this battle soon, he would lose it. Even his magnificent vitality could not take much more punishment. His balled, heavy fists whistling through the air, he struck out at the blurred figure. But to no avail!

"Somethin's wrong," growled Grrff the Xombolian, squeezing Kurdi's slender shoulder. The boy strove to see through the blurred, flying fists.

Something was indeed wrong. Ganelon's blows seemed well aimed, but somehow they were failing to connect with the body of his opponent. Zaar ducked and bobbed and weaved from side to side, but, whereas his every blow landed like a sledgehammer, pounding Silvermane's bruised and bloody torso to a pulp, the silver-haired giant seemed unable to retaliate.

True, one of his eyes was half-closed by a powerful right, and a small cut leaked mingled blood and sweat into the other, doubtless to the impairment of his vision, but still and all, by the law of averages alone, at least *some* of his mighty blows ought to have landed on the Warlord's flesh.

The boy writhed in an agony of suspense, and his hands closed upon the talisman he wore.

He was an Iomagoth, was little Kurdi, and they have little to do with the gods of other races, and few gods of their own. So the talisman he wore was not his, but had belonged to Palensus Choy: Kurdi had taken it, more or less as a souvenir, and now, lacking any gods of his own to pray to, he prayed to the divinity whose likeness he wore.

The talisman was of Ukwukluk, and it is the unique property of Ukwukluk to dispel illusions.

Perhaps it was the fervor of the lad's prayer, or the unselfishness with which he prayed, or the sincerity in his heart. Or mayhap it was, simply, that Ukwukluk, like many another godling of Gondwane the Great, appreciates good sportsmanship and disapproves of cheating.

At any rate, as Kurdi clung to the talisman and prayed as he had never prayed before—something happened.

A dazzle—a flickering halo of light—wavered into being about the darting form of the Warlord Zaar.

All present gaped, blinked, squeezed their eyes shut, then looked again.

For a split-second it seemed that there were two Zaars who circled the staggering Silvermane, pummeling him with terrible blows.

Then there was only one, the other melting into thin air.

And, in the same moment, Kishtu shrieked and clutched at his wrist, and tore therefrom the small silver charm he wore there.

He ripped it from him and threw it to the tiled floor, where it lay, smoking and spitting sparks.

Ganelon shook his head blearily, to clear his vision, and saw Zaar before him, and flung a powerful left at his unprotected belly.

Zaar surely saw the blow, but ignored it, and made no attempt to dodge the blow or to block it. It was almost as if he had some reason to suspect the blow could not land.

But it did, and such was the force of the blow that Ganelon's balled fist sank into the Warlord's belly to the wrist.

Zaar turned white as milk, then greenish. The air whistled from his lungs and he doubled over.

Taking a stand, Ganelon swung a sizzling right to his jaw. All of the might and power of those steely thews of chest, back, arm and shoulder he poured into that terrific blow. His iron fist came swinging up from his knees, to strike Zaar's jaw like a sledgehammer.

The Warlord's head snapped back. His mouth sagged open, spitting broken teeth and drooling blood.

The impact of Ganelon's right jerked him inches into the air. He fell backward, measuring his full length on the floor.

Nor did he rise again.

The Warchiefs gathered around their fallen master. Ganelon's fist had broken the jaw of Zaar in three places. And his skull, striking the stone tiles, had cracked.

Zaar the Warlord was dead.

More than a few of the Ximchaks had noticed without understanding it the curious momentary illusion that Silvermane had been fighting *two opponents*, not one.

The strange multiplicity of images was swiftly explained when Harukh Irongrim examined the smoking, still-hot talisman Kishtu had torn from his wrist.

"This is an Oomish charm," he declared harshly, "for creating the illusion that a man is where he is not. Have any here a countertalisman? A charm of Vush or Zugg or Ukwukluk?"

Kurdi timidly raised his hand. A little gentle questioning elicited from the boy that, even in the very moment the strange occurrence had happened, he had been holding the talisman, beseeching its divinity to help his giant friend.

"The mystery is solved, then," said Harukh sternly. "The shaman Kishtu, by his magic, made it seem to all of us—especially to Ganelon Silvermane—that his opponent was where he was not. That explains why the chieftain could not seem to land a blow on him, although his fists seemed to strike true.

"I declare Ganelon Silvermane, chieftain of the Kuzak Tribe of the Clan Gurko, the winner of this contest. Even had Zaar, the former Warlord, survived that last blow, I would have declared for Silvermane, for by the use of magic in defiance of Horde law, Zaar Xodensson forfeited the contest. Seize that man there!"

Guards grabbed Kishtu just as the shaman was about to slink into the shadows of the nearer column. He squeaked, whimpering for pardon.

"What say you all, my lords, to my judgment? Lord Barzik?"

"Aye."

"Lord Ulfwyn?"

"Aye."

"Lord Erkon—Lord Ovvo?"

"Aye!"

"Very well, then. Guards, convene an execution squad—bowmen, I think. Conduct Black Unggo, the shaman Kishtu, and subchief Iquanux thither. With your permission, Sire."

"Eh?" mumbled Ganelon dizzily.

"With your permission, Sire, we will speedily dispatch the three assassins. We require your permission."

"Oh," said Ganelon. Then he nodded his head, and leaned back, letting Kurdi and Grrff continue sponging the blood from his bruised and aching torso, while Grrff went back to pouring cold red wine into him.

When they had restored him to a groggy and stiff-muscled semblance of his former self, they helped Ganelon ascend the dais and seat himself in the throne of Zaar.

Then, one by one, the Warchiefs of the Nine Clans went forward to kneel before the throne, to lay their swords at Silvermane's feet, and to swear fealty to him as true and unquestioned Warlord.

Barzik of the Gurkoes was first to do so, followed by Ruzik of the Tharradians, Dygoth of the Rooxas, Ulfwyn of the Gurzimen, Erkon and Arnhelm and Ovvo and the others.

As each Warchief made his vow, Ganelon accepted it by returning his sword to him.

After the Warchiefs had sworn their loyalty to Silvermane, the chieftains of the tribes did so, followed by the subchiefs.

When Wolf Turgo knelt to swear obedience, he winked solemnly up into Silvermane's bruised, puffy face, and grinned with secret delight.

Then it was done. On the morrow, Silvermane would review the full Horde assembled, save for those in distant garrisons, but for now the ceremony was done. He wanted a hot bath to soak in, did Silvermane, and a solid supper, and a soft bed.

Maybe he was Warlord, but right now he felt more like a well-used punching bag. So woozy and dazed was he still that when the captain of the execution squad brought before him the severed heads of Black Unggo, Iquanux, and the shaman Kishtu, he did not even feel squeamish as he looked at the gory objects, but commanded they be buried along with the corpse of Zaar.

"I declare this Council closed. Tomorrow, after I review the troops and receive their allegiance, we shall reconvene to reach the decision herein deferred. You are all excused. Grrff, Kurdi, help me to my quarters. Good night to you all, my Lords," said Ganelon Silvermane, the Warlord of the Ximchak Horde.

Book Three
THE GREAT XIMCHAK MIGRATION

The Scene: Labrys and the Vigola Pass; Ong, Posch, Lake Xor and Pathon Thad; the Badlands of the Upper Arzenia; Vlith, Ruxor, the Uskodian Plain, and Pardoga.

New Characters: The Hoppers, the Weavers of Pathon Thad, and the Petrified Ruxorians; Prince Pergamon and other Pardogamen; the Strange Little Men of the Hills.

11.

ECONOMICS OF SILVERMANE

The following few days, Ganelon rested, exercised the stiffness from his lame muscles, and let the Gompish physicians fuss and fidget with his cuts, bruises, and injuries.

The first thing he had to do was to consolidate his power base. The Gurkoes were largely with him, and Lord Barzik, the Warchief, and Harukh Irongrim, the senior tribal chieftain, were among his most loyal friends and supporters. So, too, were Wolf Turgo (now, upon the execution of Black Unggo, newly elevated to the chieftaincy of the Farz) and Harsha of the Horn. Even Yargash and Larx had become good friends with him, by this point.

But to the other Clans he was still largely a stranger, much the outsider, despite the popularity he had won in the winning of the Grand Championship of the Horde.

The first thing he did was to create a personal guard, made up of the stalwarts of his own tribe, the Kuzaks. These hand-picked warriors assumed the guardianship of the Barzoolian Palace, now Ganelon's official residence, replacing Zaar's own guards.

Then he formed a personal retinue made up of the Clan champions whom he had bested during the Games. The

warm admiration and comradeship with which Bargon the
Kazooli and Tharg of Tharrad had greeted him during the
ill-fated expedition to the Pergode Pass had given Silvermane
to realize that true sportsmanship was to be found, even
among Barbarians.

So he dispatched Harsha of the Horn, now his personal
Herald and messenger, with invitations to Bargon and the
other Clan champions to join his retinue in Jurago. Very
quickly did these worthies respond, and in no time at all he
had gathered around him Varax the Gurziman, Jumba of the
Hoys, Khon the Rooxa, Nabbad of the Qarrs, Partha the Fartha, and Yurkham the Urziki. Tharg of Tharrad, of course,
was a Kuzak, and had already been invited to join the retinue
of the new Warlord.

These men donned new war-harness of a unique design,
and sported upon the breast of their jerkins enameled badges
emblematic of the nine-plume headdress Ganelon wore as
Grand Champion. Very shortly thereafter, within the first two
weeks of the new Warlord's reign, the "Nine Champions" as
they were called (Ganelon being included therein) formed a
distinctive new class of Horde nobility, and not a man among
them but was proud of the honor of membership.

This honor, of course, reflected back upon the Clans they
had left to join the Warlord's guard: and in this way Ganelon
mollified the remnants of hostility he detected among the
other Clans than his own, and courted their friendship.

Two weeks to the day after he was proclaimed Warlord,
Ganelon feasted the Champions in high honor, an event to
which each of the Clan Warchiefs and their senior tribal
chieftain attended, so as to witness the high regard and esteem the new Warlord felt for the Champions he had bested,
and had now made his boon companions and closest friends.

They went away that night pleased and flattered—as had
been Silvermane's intention from the first.

Three days later, Ganelon convened the Council of the
Warchiefs, tribal chieftains and their subchiefs, to resume discussion of their route out of Gompery.

Instead of negotiating as Zaar had done, Ganelon convened the Great Council in order to present its members with
his decision. It seemed likely to him that the chiefs wanted

their Warlord to be a man of firm, unalterable decision—a true leader.

"It is my plan to lead the Horde out of Gompia through the Vigola Pass and thus directly west," he explained. "You will notice from the chart on this stand, my Lords, that the Vigola is several leagues north of the Marjid. The route I wish to take, which is drawn here in crimson, skirts the Mad Empire of Trancore to the north and does not molest its borders."

"But, Sire, will not the Trancorians attack in that flying fortress of theirs, inflicting upon us another defeat as disastrous as that we suffered on the Ovarva Plains?" objected Erkon, Warchief of the Hoys.

"Not so, Lord Erkon," said Ganelon decisively. "You perhaps forget that the Flying Palace of Zaradon, which decimated the Gurko Clan upon those plains, is under the control of my former associate, the Immortal Palensus Choy."

"So?" shrugged the Hoy. "Now that you have shifted your allegiance and become a Ximchak, doubtless the magician will count you among his enemies, and will consider the northwestern migration of the Horde as nothing more than a flanking action—an attempt on our part to take Trancore unawares, invading from the north."

"Not so, I say again," said Ganelon. "For I will send a message to Palensus Choy under my own name and in my own hand, informing him that I intend to lead the Horde directly into the west, avoiding Trancore entirely, and, by so doing, removing for all time to come the peril in which Trancore currently stands from the Ximchak occupation of Gompery."

"And how, Sire, do you expect to get this message through to your former magician friend?" inquired Dygoth, Warchief of the Rooxas.

"By means of my ally, Ishgadara," said Silvermane. "The sphinx-girl, as you know, can fly to Zaradon and back with Choy's reply in a day or two."

"Hrmph," grunted Erkon of the Hoys. He exchanged a glance with Dygoth the Rooxa, then they grimaced, subsiding. Ganelon had well thought this one through, they decided.

"To leave Gompery by the north—is this not to retreat?" growled Saphur of Qarr.

Ganelon shook his head. "How so, Lord Saphur? It was not by the Vigola Pass that the Horde entered Gompery two and a half years ago, or whenever it was, but by the Xuru Pass up here at the northernmost part of the mountains. To retreat is to go out the same way you came in. We are only choosing one of several alternate routes to exit from the Regime of the Gomps. No stigma can possibly be attached to this action."

"Well, for my part, Sire, I wonder why you choose the Vigola Pass and this westerly route at all?" asked Barzik, Warchief of the Gurkoes. "What is there for us to conquer? Only forests and hills and grasslands, from the map."

"In order to conquer, warriors must eat," Ganelon reminded him. "And the Horde is starving, or soon will be. The forests are filled with game, and the hills and grasslands are heavy with herds of wild cattle. This I know, for Ishgadara has been scouting that route for me over the past few days. Surely, the Ximchaks have not so soon forgotten the skills of their fathers, who were nomad bands and tribes of wandering hunters before Xoden the Warlord arose to rouse them from their pleasantly pastoral mode of existence. Surely, we can still hunt!"

"Um," said Barzik, unable to think of a rejoinder.

There ensued a little more discussion of the matter, but not very much. In essence, the problem was a simple one: how to get out of Gompia before they had to start eating the Gomps. There were only nine passages through the ring of mountains which encircled the Gompish Regime, and the three southern passes were considered hopeless, because the Flying Castle of Zaradon, having already prevented one southward thrust therethrough, could be presumed to block a second. The three eastern passes, like the Pergode, led into the burning wastes of the impassable Xoroth Desert. The pass to the north, the Xuru, was beyond use, as to employ it would be to truly retreat, thus admitting to all that the Horde had been defeated by nature itself.

Only two passes led directly into the west, and, of those, the Marjid was very obviously blocked by Zaradon.

There was really no other way out, save by the Vigola. And so it was decided.

Leaving the Barzoolian Palace upon the termination of the Council, the Warchiefs felt in general rather satisfied with the manner in which Ganelon Silvermane had conducted himself during this first key test of his leadership abilities. They agreed that he had swiftly reached the only tenable solution to the impasse, and had countered all objections to his plan reasonably and even intelligently.

It had been in this particular area that the former Warlord had failed them to some degree. A brilliant war leader, a military genius, Zaar had few gifts for diplomacy, argument, persuasion, or councilmanship in general.

"Now, if the lad—*hrrmph!*—the Warlord, that is, be only half as good at leading us in battle as he is at the council table, we have found ourselves a true winner," mused Ruzik of the Tharradians amiably.

"Aye, there is that," nodded Ovvo Redtooth, Warchief of the Farthamen. "I've a notion we'll soon find out."

"How so?" inquired Ruzik.

Ovvo shrugged. "Once we've shaken the mud o' Gompery off'n our heels, there's all the west to ravage, loot 'n' plunder," he pointed out. "And, doubtless, some folks already got there ahead o' us, an'll be hot to contest us for it."

"Ah!" grinned Lord Ruzik, feeling cheerful at the prospects. There was nothing more dear to a Ximchak's heart than the promise of a good, bloody battle. And Ruzik of Tharrad was a Ximchak to his toes.

But Ganelon, of course, wasn't. He had *become* a Ximchak by adoption and by choice: but that did not imply that he had taken Ximchak ways to heart. He had neither adopted their careless disregard for the property rights of others, nor had he chosen to follow their warlike ways. He was determined to somehow wean them to his somewhat more civilized respect for other nations that were not Ximchak.

In this, he could foresee many problems. But his first step was well taken: the westerly route he planned to conduct the Horde on was happily a route which led through mostly uninhabited lands.

Preparations for the departure were underway immediately, but it was not all that simple or easy to uproot a couple of hundred thousand warriors overnight. Some of them had taken wives from among the Gompish women, and others had taken slaves. Ganelon was anxious to leave the poor miserable Gomps with what little they had left, so he passed a rule that wives could accompany the Horde while slaves could not.

In answer to the anguished howls of those who had accumulated a harem or a household of slaves, he pointed out that there was little enough food left for the Ximchaks alone, much less for thousands of slaves. So the slaves were left behind.

He passed the same sort of rule about loot and plunder. The treasures looted from the palaces and mansions of the Gomps were too heavy and bulky to transport, he argued. Carrying all that gold and silver and gems—to say nothing of the marble statues, the tapestries and rare carpets and rich brocades—would slow the Horde considerably on its march into the west. Ximchak children and oldsters would die of starvation or malnutrition, he pointed out, while the Horde lumbered heavily along, under the crushing burden of mountains of loot.

You cannot eat gold, he taught his troops, and it is among the heaviest of metals.

Grumbling and grexing, the Ximchaks followed his advice, although it pierced them to the heart to leave so much costly plunder behind. But even the densest of the Horde could see the logic behind Silvermane's reasoning.

"This here new Warlord o' ours be just too dang smart fer his own good," complained Arnhelm Blackshield of the Kazooli. "Leavin' all thet thar plunder ahind, well, hit just ain't th' Ximchak way!"

When the Kazooli gripe was reported to him, Ganelon grimly suggested that, in order to survive in these parts of the world, it might well prove necessary for the Ximchaks to learn new ways.

It was a promise he intended to make come true, if he could.

And so, slowly, over the next few weeks, the Horde gradually gathered on the plains before Labrys, one of the more northerly of the Thirty Cities, which guarded the entrance to the Vigola Pass. Garrison by garrison was emptied; hunting parties and patrols were called in; tribe by tribe, the mighty Clans moved north for the migration.

In all, it took a good seven weeks for the entire Horde to assemble before Labrys. And the last city to be left ungarrisoned was Jurago itself. Just before quitting the capital, Ganelon conducted a brief, hasty ceremony to which he summoned the surviving lords and nobles of the Regime.

He then in their presence crowned Princess Ruzara as the Regina Plutarchus of All the Gomps.

Actually, the coronation was not exactly a coronation. Since kings wear crowns, and the Gomps have no kings, there was no need to "coronate" anybody. The equivalent was interesting and probably unique.

Since the Gomps worship wealth above everything, the ceremony of investiture involved pouring a shower of gold coins in the lap of the monarch. The gleam of that golden shower awoke a similar gleam of cupidity in the eyes of the Gompish courtiers. These Ximchaks, they seemed to be thinking, were not such bad fellows after all!

Ganelon then made a short speech in which he restored the sovereignty of Gompland to the new Gompish sovereign. Then he left, taking the Champions and his Kuzaks with him, leaving the Regina Ruzara on the throne beside her sister.

It could not be denied that Silvermane was a most economical Warlord: as yet, even the loudest grumblers among the Ximchaks had no reason to suspect him of being a peace-lover. With impeccable logic he had trimmed the Horde of its loot and plunder and slaves and most of its women, leaving the Gomps with most of what had been taken away from them, thus making the Horde lighter and the Gomps happy.

Tribe by tribe, the Clans marched through the Vigola into the forestlands north of Trancore. There were no attacks, and no holdups. Everything moved smoothly.

But in Jurago, things were not so smooth. Ruzara raved and wept within her royal apartments, to the bewilderment of Mavella. The calm blond girl could not understand the storms raging within the heart of that tempestuous tomboy, her sister. It seemed to Mavella that with the Horde withdrawn from their realm, and the long ordeal of the occupation over, the Regina should have been as relieved and happy as were her people, who were dancing in the streets in celebration of the two joyful events—the retreat of the hated Ximchaks and the restoration of the House of Tharzash.

Ruzara simply couldn't explain her emotions, even to herself. Until the Ximchaks came roaring and ravaging and rampaging down from the north to turn everything on its ear, the girl had never realized how placid and boring her life had been. She had never really enjoyed life with zest and appetite, until the Conquest. And now, with the Horde gone, life would return to normal—that is, from her point of view, to a sort of insipid boredom.

She could hardly endure the notion. With the withdrawal of the last Ximchak units, it seemed to her that everything in her life that was lively and vivid and dangerous and exciting was also ebbing away, leaving the calm dullness of the shallows in place of the vigorous turmoil of the stormy seas. (If the metaphor seems a trifle labored, you must excuse Ruzara: she was really quite upset.)

And then there was the question of Ganelon Silvermane, for whom she had conceived an intense and violent and still unsatisfied passion. In the two months and more since he had wrested the mastery of the Ximchaks from Zaar, she had seen much of him, but not as much as she desired. Nothing she had done had gained his attention: he ignored her flirting, or seemed oblivious to it, passed up invitations for private rides and walks and tête-à-têtes, and hardly ever had she managed to be alone with the stalwart young giant.

He had no other women, as far as she had been able to find out, and the ease with which he resisted her blandishments infuriated her, even as it baffled her.

Without Ganelon, she would eventually be forced to mate with some fat, greasy little Gompish princeling whose main passion in life was his greed for gold. The thought was sickening.

Mavella tried to sooth and calm her stormy tears, but Ruzara would not be pacified. Abruptly, she dismissed her sister, saying she wished to be left alone.

The next morning she was gone, and so were her Ximchak raiment and gear and the fleetest ornith left in the stables.

In her place was only a letter—a brief note scribbled in purple ink, which read as follows:

WE, RUZARA II, Regina Plutarchus of the Tharzashian Dynasty, herewith renounce all claim to the Gompish Throne for Us and the Heirs of Our Body forever. We Abdicate in favor of Our Royal Sister, Mavella.

Ruzara R. P.

Writ in Our Own Hand this 10th chopac, 4th xad, Zome 241, of the Scarlet Epoch.

To which there was appended a briefer and even less formal note, to wit:

Forgive me, dear Sister! You will make a better Regina for Gompery than I ever could. I go to live the life I long for, beside the man I love.

And it was signed:

Ruzara of the Horde.

12.

ONG, POSCH, AND THE PETRIFIED CITY

Beyond the Vigola Pass the Horde entered upon a region of meadowland called Ong.

Here roamed immense flocks of lumbering cattle called nerds. For a time the Ximchaks reverted to the ways of their nomadic forebears, and hunted the nerd herds day and night. The meat of these beasts, although tender and delicious, was colored a delicate shade of pale green, probably from the habitual nerd tendency to feed upon the meadow grasses.

No humans or near-humans inhabited these meadowlands, but they were infested by Hoppers, as was soon discovered.

Hoppers are a skinny, ungainly mammalian life form with long, agile legs, bald heads, huge, goblinlike eyes and ears. Slightly intelligent, they lived by preying upon the herds of nerds, and by begging from travelers.

Because of their long, double-kneed legs, they were able to leap about like jack rabbits or grasshoppers, which made it hard to catch them and harder still to chase them. They would leap into a Ximchak camp, snatch up a steaming cookpot or whatever seized their fancy, then leap the barricades again. Like jackdaws, the Hoppers collected curiosities, as well as edibles. A Hopper nest, when uncovered, might hold seashells, colored pebbles, pieces of old metal, rags of vivid cloth, and sometimes gems or jewelry.

They were more of a nuisance than anything else, and Ganelon outlawed the killing of the harmless pranksters.

Decimating the nerd herds, the Ximchaks passed on. For the three weeks it took them to traverse the Ongish plains, they ate heavily, although monotonously, of nerd steaks, nerd cutlet, nerd stew, spiced nerd, pickled nerd, minced nerd, and nerd soup. Long before leaving Ong, they were heartily weary of the very taste of nerd: it took them three weeks.

Ong was bordered to the west by the Ongadonga Mountains, steeper and more rugged than the mountains which encircled Gompia, and, unlike those mountains, there were no passes. The Horde was forced to scale the precipitous heights of the Ongadongas, and, heaving and puffing, hauling their loads of gear and provisions up the sheer cliffs by painful inches, the Horde warriors had good reason to applaud the wisdom and caution and foresight of their new Warlord in forbidding them to bring with them the spoils of Gompery. They could never have gotten them over the Ongadongas.

Beyond the mountains they entered a region called Posch, which was rather heavily forested.

Here they fed on game birds, flying fish, a curious species of perambulating vegetable called the Posch squash, and some delicious fruits and berries for which the groves of Posch were famous.

The crossing of Posch took them the better part of two weeks.

The change in diet was extremely welcome, but the novelty of the foodstuffs of Posch occasioned some bad temper and considerable humor. The large yellow gourdlike vegetables, for instance, were exceptionally tasty, but wary of humans and fleet of foot.

Or, rather, fleet of *root*, not foot. The vegetables had, over the ages, for some reason evolved into self-mobile condition, and traveled about by means of coiled, tough, wriggling, hairy roots, which squirmed and jiggled along, hunting for underground sources of water. When the Posch squash found a subterranean lake or stream, it squatted down, dug its roots into the loam, and drank thirstily.

Between these drinking times, however, the squash could negotiate the meadowland quite rapidly, and the Ximchaks chased them to and fro, sweating profusely and swearing lustily. Also, they seldom won in these contests of speed, agility, and dodging. The rest of the Poschine flora, thank Galendil, tended to stay where it was put.

The Ximchak passed due north of Trancore without molestation by the Flying Castle, and traveled beyond the limits of the Mad Empire, leaving it behind with considerable relief.

Ganelon had communicated, as he had said he would, with Palensus Choy, obtaining from the Immortal his promise not to bring the Flying Castle against the Horde as long as they respected the Trancorian borders. Ganelon saw to it that these agreements were strictly observed.

They forded the shallow Euros and the swift-flowing Huxor, and, reaching the wide river called Xorish, he had his troops build enormous rafts out of the groves of pithy, unsinkable yotzle trees, for the Xorish was navigable. They followed this river west for about six days, passing through the wooded hills of Qoy.

He did this for a reason, did Ganelon. The Forestlands of Qoy were inhabited by a race of green-skinned creatures who called themselves the Qoy Foresters. This peculiar folk worshipped the trees among which they lived and from which they considered themselves to have descended. When visited by Outlanders, they tended to fight like fury in defense of their sacred ancestral groves. For the Ximchaks to have traversed Qoy overland would have meant fighting any number of pitched battles with the Foresters, who were famous archers. The Ximchaks would probably have won out in the end through sheer weight of numbers, but the slaughter of the poor Foresters would have been ghastly. Ganelon had no wish to slay the simple, mad tree-dwellers, hence avoided the whole situation by taking the river route.

The Xorish emptied its waters into the landlocked lake called Xor, on whose shores rose a city called Pathon Thad.

The Pathon-Thadians were a friendly, peace-loving folk, famous weavers and dyers, but never given much notice in the annals of war.

Despite their unwarlike ways, however, the men of Pathon

Thad had nothing to fear even from so mighty an army as the Ximchak Horde. This was because their stone-walled city was built in the middle of Lake Xor, and the lake itself was the dwelling place of immense crustacea. These monster crabs resembled lobsters grown to the size of mastodons. The Pathon-Thadians had long ago domesticated the creatures for purposes of riding beasts, employed their secretions for a variety of colorful dyes, and used their natural combativeness in the defense of the island city.

Covered with natural armor, their twelve chitin-clad legs terminating in powerful pincerlike claws, the Xor crustacea were fearful opponents. One glimpse of them and the Ximchaks were happy to pole their rafts ashore and trek on northwest, leaving Pathon Thad unharmed and undisturbed behind them.

Just as Ganelon had hoped they would do.

Crossing the Hills of Delm, they entered Greater Zuavia's neighboring conglomerate to the west, which was called Upper Arzenia.

The Horde by this time was well fed, in fine fettle, although rather spoiling for a bit of the good old sack-and-pillage.

Unfortunately, except for Pathon Thad, which certainly had looked impregnable, there did not seem to be anything hereabouts to sack or pillage.

This was due to the carefully planned route along which Ganelon Silvermane was conducting them, although the Ximchaks had no reason to suspect it. Guided by Ishgadara's daily reconnaissance flights, Ganelon was carefully steering his charges between centers of civilization, trying to avoid warfare as far as was possible.

Thus it chanced that they passed just below the kingdoms of Torx, Havanor and Quee, and just above the realms of Porchavoy, Ibb, and Amaramara. They were traveling through the Badlands, unknown to them, carefully skirting the civilized countries which lay along their route. Ganelon figured that what the Ximchaks didn't know couldn't hurt them.

He was having considerable trouble with Ruzara.

She had caught up with the rear guard of the Horde while

they were still working their way across the meadowlands of Ong.

Brought before the Warlord, she explained that she had abdicated the Reginaship of Gompland and desired to join the Ximchaks.

Warrior girls were something new to the Barbarians, for, although they had heard of the girl knights of Jemmerdy, the Warrior Women of Khond, and the Red Amazons of the Cham Archipelago in their travels, they had heretofore managed to avoid any actual contact with any of the fighting female races.*

However, they were well acquainted with Ruzara by now, and knew her to be a feisty lass with a taste for bloodletting, a fondness for the life of camp and field, and a nifty knack for archery. So they prevailed upon the Warlord to let her stay.

Ganelon was against the whole idea, but finally said it was all right with him, since it was all right with everyone else. It would hardly do for him to officially oppose the recruitment of strangers, since he himself had entered the Horde that same way. Nevertheless, he tried to avoid encountering Ruzara as much as he could. Her languishing looks, gusty sighs, and the husky, seductive tones that entered her voice whenever she spoke to him made him distinctly uncomfortable.

Grrff the Xombolian noted this, and chuckled to himself. It was not the first time a good-looking girl had fallen for the big man, and probably would not be the last. Grrff went back far enough to remember the Sirix Xarda of Jemmerdy, to say nothing of Zelmarine the Red Enchantress. If Ganelon had not yielded to those two (very different) beauties, he was not likely to succumb to the wiles and blandishments of Ruzara, despite the vivid appeal of the attractive Gomp girl.

It was not that Ganelon Silvermane was immune to the

---

* They just missed a clash with the Khondites, apparently. The Warrior Women inhabit the snowy uplands of the northern parts of Lesser Zuavia, just beyond the Thu Mountains which border the upper edges of the Xoroth desertlands. If the Ximchaks had passed up their chance to go down through the Xuru Pass into Gompia, and continued a few hundred miles, they would have found themselves smack in the middle of Khond, and probably fighting for their very lives.

charms of women, or preferred some other gender or species. A synthetic man, constructed in a breeding vat by the genetic skills of the Time Gods, he had been "born," as it were, fully grown, but with the mentality of an infant.

He had learned swiftly, acquiring a superficial veneer of apparent maturity. After all, he had the intellectual equipment and capacity of an adult. But as for his emotional development, well, that was a matter of inner growth and cumulative experience, and could not be measured by inches or by years.

Physically, Ganelon was mature. Chronologically, he was only about four years old. And emotionally—sexually—he was still in the prepubescent state of a little boy scarcely twelve.

No wonder Ruzara got nowhere with him!

It took the Horde two days to reach the Hills of Delm and the borders of Upper Arzenia, four days to cross the hill country, and they were three weeks passing through the Badlands.

By the time they came out of the Badlands, they had been ten weeks on the Great Migration, and everything had shaken down into place. The fleet-footed orniths and the heavy, lumbering nguamadons who hauled the wains full of tentage and camp gear were doing well: all of the beasts who were sickly or lame had either died or been left behind. As for the warriors, the rough, hardy life of road and camp and cross-country march had toughened them up, sweating off the flab accumulated by soft city life. A new, richer, more varied diet—and a plentiful one, at that—had restored them to their clear-eyed, vigorous selves.

They were in fine fettle, and their morale was never higher. While it was true, to their disgruntlement, they had as yet fought no battles, besieged no cities, nor laid waste to any kingdoms, at least they had lost few men to fever, snakebite, wild beasts, or savages.

It was good to be on the march again, after nearly three years of sitting around doing nothing in Gompland, and getting bored with it.

They approached the Rlambar Mountains, worked their way through the Hu Pass, and marched through Vlith and across the broad Uskodian Plain. It took them thirty days to do this, and while traversing Vlith or perhaps the Plain, there passed by unnoticed by any the anniversary of Ganelon's first year among the Ximchaks.

By the end of that time they had reached the suburbs of fabulous Ruxor, the one of the many marvels of the Conglomerate of Upper Arzenia. Like many another band of tourists who had passed by this route, the Ximchaks stopped to have a look at the famous Petrified City.

Ganelon had heard vaguely of it from the Illusionist's library of curious occult tomes back home in Nerelon. And the Ximchaks had picked up vague, distorted accounts of it during their travels, which amounted to little more than rumor and legend. It was interesting to view the thing in person: it was, after all, one of the most celebrated of the many marvels of Gondwane the Great.

It lay before them, bathed in the clear gold brilliance of dawn, a splendid metropolis of gleaming snow-white stone. It had lain thus uninhabited for more centuries than any of them could count, and yet (and this was strange) time had not eroded its beauties or impaired the symmetry of its many spires and domes.

The city had originally been built by wandering tribes of Ruxmen, fled from their homeland so as to be able to practice their religion unmolested. That religion was the worship of Rux, one of the less popular and more controversial divinities of the old Vemenoid Pantheon.

They had built the city of the red Uskodian granite and decorated it with the rich amber-yellow marbles quarried from the Rlambar foothills. But now everything in the city of Ruxor was of gleaming, sleek, sparkling white stone.

Including the Ruxorians. For they were still there, with their cattle and housepets and windowboxes and walled gardens and tree-lined streets: all transformed to the same white stone in the same mysterious moment.

It had come out of the depths of space, according to the *Annals of Arzenia*, that weird and terrifying beam of purple light which had originated, according to some accounts, in the Constellation of the Mantichore.

For one eternal instant of time, the space ray had bathed

red-and-golden Ruxor in its uncanny purple radiance: then it flashed on to strike, perhaps, another distant world.

Whatever the nature of the weird purple light, it struck everything in Ruxor to stone in the same instant.

Strolling through the gleaming white streets of Ruxor was like something experienced in a dream.

The Ruxorians had been petrified while busied about their ordinary tasks. The women were hanging out the washing, or sweeping off the doorstep, or cooking a meal, or entertaining a lover.

The children were playing in the streets, chasing hoops and throwing balls and playing with small domestic animals, or being spanked, or stealing apples, or taking naps.

The priests were officiating before the altars of Rux. The Civic Guard was patrolling the streets, guarding the gates, snoozing off-duty in the barracks, dicing behind the latrines, or flirting with the girls.

Merchants squatted beneath striped awnings in the bazaar, or haggled over booths, or sipped fayowaddy tea complacently, to celebrate a sale.

Scribes scribbled with stone pens on stone parchments. Moneylenders weighed stone bags of stone coins in stone balances. Jewelers scrutinized stone gems through opaque stone lenses. Stone weavers toiled at stone looms, weaving threads of stone.

By a horse water trough in the forum, a stone dog had been petrified in mid-wee, one stone leg lifted.

It was weird beyond my gifts to describe.

And no one knew how or why it had happened.

The Horde moved on at sunset, and camped over the borders of Pardoga.

And they finally found a little of the excitement they had been looking for.

13.

THE SLEEPING FOREST

Pardoga was a rocky land of many hills and dense, thickly grown forests.

It took the Horde two full days, after leaving the Petrified City, to penetrate the borders of Pardoga.

They made camp that second evening just within the cool green glades of a quiet forest.

Wind murmured through the long, drooping fronds of green-and-silver trees not unlike weeping willows. The breeze whispered soothingly through long, twisting, ribbonlike leaves.

Small streams gurgled drowsily, pouring their glistening waters over rounded stones.

It was all very restful. Maybe just a little too restful.

Kurdi was the first to notice something strange about the forest. The little boy had thrived during the three months and two weeks of the Great Migration. The fresh air, the warm sunlight, the exercise, the good food, all these had put a sparkle in his eye and roses in his cheeks, as the saying goes. He was tanned and fit, and seemed to have grown a couple of inches.

Everything that had happened thus far was new and excit-

110

ing to the boy, and he greeted everything with zest and appetite, eager for new experiences and new adventures.

The passage across the rocky borders of Pardoga had been rough going, but, while the men were weary enough and ready to sleep, Kurdi was still hopping with restless energy. He would in fact have volunteered for sentry-go, had it not been that, as the squire of the Warlord, the boy was excused from other duties.

But he just couldn't get to sleep. His mind was too active, his imagination too lively. He kept expecting something to pop out of the bushes and come roaring and ramping at them—something huge and pink, with yellow spots, perhaps, and eighteen eyes, or maybe eighteen horns.

There was something about this forest that puzzled him, but he couldn't quite figure out what it was.

Maybe it was the sleepy, soothing murmur of the water gliding over the round rocks, or the languid way the long ribbony leaves of the graceful, drooping trees drifted in the warm, perfumed breeze.

And then it hit him.

There was no life in the forest: none at all.

He jumped up, ears tingling with excitement, peering around him through the green-and-golden twilight which bathed the dreaming glade.

Kurdi had seen plenty of forests since he had first left Kan Zar Kan to go adventuring with Ganelon Silvermane. He remembered the jungles of Nimboland, and the Urrach forest east of Trancore, and all the forests of Ong and Posch through which they had more recently journeyed, to say nothing of the Badlands.

In all of the forests he had ever known there had been wild beasts and birds, and little scurrying creatures of the small, inoffensive sort. Rabbits and squirrels and field mice, anyway, were to be expected (or the Gondwanish equivalents of such small rodents, that is), if not such exotic creatures as the Hoppers or those odd and interesting flying fish they had back in Posch.

But there was nothing cheeping in the grasses, or rustling in the underbrush or chirping from the branches of THIS forest!

111

And that meant, there was something wrong. Something *very* wrong.

In Gondwane the Great, in the Twilight of Time, when the small, scuttling forest creatures desert a forest, you can be sure there is something seriously wrong with that forest.

Kurdi scampered up to the nearest sentry, a tall, rather friendly young Urzik named Cartha who had always been one of Kurdi's particular favorites, and had been teaching him the fine arts of knife-fighting in his off-duty hours.

The tall, chocolate-skinned Urzik leaned heavily on his feather-tufted spear, his head bowed on his chest. He seemed to be fast asleep, and did not rouse himself when Kurdi called his name or tugged on his jerkin, nor even when the boy, gathering his courage, hauled back and kicked him sharply in the shins.

Kurdi's eyes bugged wide and his heart began to beat faster and faster. Something was happening here, and whatever it was, it was wrong, *terribly* wrong. Because Ximchak sentries did not sleep while on guard; not ever. And especially, they did not fall so soundly to sleep before it was even dark, after being on guard for less than half an hour.

Catching his breath in something that sounded suspiciously like a sob, Kurdi ran back into the camp and tried to rouse his friends.

The Kuzaks and the Champions had drawn their bedrolls up in a wide circle around the huge tent wherein the Warlord took his rest. They occupied that particular glade of the forest, with the Gurkoes encamped to their left, the Kazoolies to the right, and the Hoys directly behind them, near the edges of the mysterious forest. The rest of the Horde was scattered away to either side.

The forest was immensely huge, and blocked this entrance into Pardoga so that you had to go through it to enter into Pardoga proper. It had seemed to Ganelon Silvermane the best thing to do was camp in the forest, and wait till daylight to continue farther into the groves.

He would probably have decided to camp on the plain before the forest, if there had been a plain before the forest, which there was not. There was only acre after acre of rough, broken, uneven, rock-strewn ground, crawling with small blind red serpents—about the worse, and most uncomfortable, campground imaginable: hence, he had chosen to camp in the forest, which seemed quiet and peaceful.

Well, now it was even quieter than before.

The sleeping Kuzaks were so deep in their slumbers that they weren't even snoring. Kurdi tried to wake them up, tugging and pulling and yelling himself hoarse, but nothing happened. They slept as soundly as if they had all been drugged.

Kurdi began to be really scared by now. This was distinctly unnatural, even ominous. He wondered if some malefic sorcerer, unbeknown to them all, had observed the warlike array of men and riding beasts and pack animals filing into Pardoga, and had hurled his wizardry upon them for some reason known only to himself.

It seemed dreadfully possible: surely, nothing this side of witchcraft could account for the unnatural slumber which gripped the Ximchaks.

Kurdi clutched the Ukwukluk talisman he still wore around his neck on a thong, and tried to think of something to do. It occurred to the boy that the talisman might well have protective powers beyond those he already knew about: this might very well explain why he remained awake, while all the Horde slept around him a deathlike, tranced sleep.

During the next two hours, Kurdi proved to himself that his direst fears were true.

Ganelon Silvermane, yes, even that mighty champion, slept on his bed of Youk-furs, and his slumbers were so deep that nothing Kurdi could do could break them.

Grrff the Xombolian and Ishgadara the Gynosphinx also slept like the dead.

So also slept the brawny Champions, all eight of them, stretched out in a row like cadavers on a row of mortuary slabs.

To the left of the Zukak encampment, Kurdi had ventured among the slumbering Gurkoes, finding them as soundly locked in the same enchanted sleep as everyone else.

He went to the right of the glade in which the Kuzaks were encamped, and found the Kazool Clan sleeping under similar circumstances. He even pushed his way through the bushes to the rear, and explored the camp of the Hoys.

Everybody seemed to be under the same evil spell. Kurdi

did not bother to investigate the sleeping places of the other Clans and tribes; that would have taken hours, and there was no doubt left in his mind by this time that he would find them deep in the same strange, enchanted sleep that had fallen upon everyone.

Except for him.

The Pardogamen were well aware that a mighty force of armed Barbarians had been streaming across their borders out of the Uskodian Plain for the past two days.

The sentinels of Pardoga rely upon trained hawks, who can fly higher than a man could climb, see farther than any man can see, and never fall asleep on guard duty.

These hawks are larger than most birds, and more intelligent. Their glistening azure plumage and white-crested heads are very nearly invisible against the dark-blue skies of Old Earth in this age, and they can easily ascend to such a height that men can hardly see them from beneath.

Trained over centuries to watch for unexpected or illegal things, they have the task of guarding the borders of Pardoga. Thus, when the hawk patrols sighted the first opening wedge of the immense Barbarian incursion into this realm, and flew to Sargish, the capital, with the news, the Pardogamen were fully apprised of the invasion before it was barely underway.

Prince Pergamon, the ruler of Sargish and Overlord of all of the Seven Baronies of Pardoga, was seated in the tall tower of his palace, playing at skittles with one of his knights, Sir Berglamum.

The Prince was lean, slim, long-legged, with clever eyes, a sharp, mocking laugh, and a smirking, thin-lipped mouth. He was witty, given to sardonic humor, and very fond of playing skittles.

Sir Berglamum the Bluff, to give him his full agnomen, was old and gray and getting fat. He had a tremendous and very intimidating mustache, like a robber bandit in a bad movie, a glaring eye—bright green, like all Pardogamen—and he was not at all fond of skittles.

Skittles was a complicated game involving a board marked off into one hundred and thirty-seven lozenges, played with small stylized figures whittled out of skittlenuts (hence the name of the game), round ivory tokens, black rectangular markers, and a handful of slim sticks called "daws."

The game was such a complex one, with such an immense variety of potential moves, and so very many rules, that a single skittles game could take a full week to play, and often did.

The Prince had been playing this particular game with the fat old knight for nine evenings now, and Sir Berglamum was sick to death of the whole thing. He wished very sincerely that something would interrupt this infernal (and interminable) game, and give him an excuse to go somewhere else for a while until the Prince forgot all about playing it further.

Thus, when an immense blue patrol-hawk came soaring in through the tall casement windows, which had been left open for just that purpose (although the evening was fairly coolish, it being early spring in Pardoga), he jumped to his feet with a loud, satisfied *"Hah!"* and scattered the gaming-pieces across the floor with a noisy clatter.

The Prince did not bother to reprimand him, for this particular patrol-hawk was Squaa, the captain of the Border Patrol, and the untimely interruption boded affairs of momentousness and considerable importance. Because the courtiers of Sargish Palace had long ago learned never to interrupt Prince Pergamon when he was playing at skittles, unless it was something really *important*. Even the hawks knew better.

Squaa landed on the back of the tall carven chair in which Prince Pergamon had been sitting. Then, spreading his wings with a rustle of pinions, he fluttered over to one corner of the tower room, where the floor was marked off with circles and squares in an odd pattern, painted in different colors.

Catching the Prince's alert eye, the patrol-hawk scratched with his right foreclaw on a red square.

"Ah?" exclaimed the Prince. "From the southeast!"

Sir Berglamum, who had been chewing upon the ends of his magnificent mustache in an agony of suspense, spat them out, heaved a heart-felt sigh, and said: "Thanks be to the Great Guz! I feared ... something from the ... *other* direction."

This peculiar remark went without reply from the Prince, who obviously knew what the fat knight meant by it. The Prince's own relief was visible in his sharp, keen features.

The hawk now performed an odd dance, hopping first on this foot, then the other, moving from red square to green lozenge to yellow circle, tapping all the while with his long hooked beak upon a hollow plaquette suspended from the roofbeams, evidently for that very purpose.

Observing his every movement closely, the Prince read the message. It would seem that the Pardogamen and the intelligent hawks had long ago worked out a code language whereby they could communicate.

"An army of strangers, pouring over the borders from Ruxor," snapped Pergamon.

"Great Guz!"

"Many tens-or-tens-of-thousands of them," the Prince added after a moment, watching the bird's queer hopping dance and reading the meaning of his beak-taps.

"They will by tomorrow night encamp in the thousand glades of the Sleeping Forest," exclaimed the Prince with satisfaction.

"Ah, then, Sire!" huffed the old knight. "We not only have nothing to worry about, but there's no hurry in taking care of it."

"True enough, Berglamum," said the Prince quickly. "But it's best that we arrive on the scene first, to remove whatever valuables the stranger-army may possess, before the woodsmen and farmers thereabouts get wind of the visit, and pick them clean!"

"Aye, there *is* that, Sire," nodded the old knight wisely.

"Therefore," said the Prince, striding up and down the chamber, rubbing his lean, supple hands together briskly, "I bid you call out the Red Lances. And the Green Bannerets. Best we levy a sizable work force of yeomen, to carry the loot and attend to—*ah*—the other necessary work. *You* know what I mean."

"Oh, aye, Sire."

"I mean, the *burying.*"

The fat knight nodded.

"I shall ride with you, Berglamum."

The knight saluted and backed from the Presence. Clumping down the spiral staircase, he mumbled the figures to himself.

" 'Tens-of-tens-of-thousands," he repeated. "Hoy, that means at least one hundred thousand bodies—perhance even more!"

Privately, he decided to levy plenty of yeomen. One hundred thousand was a lot of graves to be dug.

By dawn of the third day after the Ximchak army began pouring across the borders into Pardoga, Prince Pergamon and his two troops of chivalry, accompanied by a glum-faced mob of several hundred unhappy yeomen, reached the southeastern edges of the Sleeping Forest.

The yeomen went in first, and gingerly, waved on by the knights. Even though they held spears, battleaxes and swords in their hands, it took a lot of waving, and more than a little cursing, to get the reluctant peasants to enter the shadowy forest.

Each yeoman wore around his neck a small scaraboid of colored paste, handed out to them by the knights. These amulets were similar in color, shape, size and composition to the talisman which little Kurdi wore around his own neck.

The yeomen returned, saying the forest had done its work and the invading army was all soundly asleep.

"Aye, and likely to stay so, until the crack o' doom!" chortled Sir Berglamum in fine good humor.

All day the yeomen, supervised by the knights in their red or green surcoats, lugged heavy bodies out of the thousand glades of the immense tract of enchanted woodland. The eyes of the knights gleamed at sight of the golden ornaments, the jewels, the fine steel weapons, the rich accouterments.

They heaped the bodies neatly in man-tall piles, row after row of them.

That evening, Prince Pergamon sat drinking beer in his silken pavilion. He was curiously examining an immense broadsword whose blade was somehow fashioned out of sparkling silver, the metal tempered by Fire Magic (he suspected) to a hardness exceeding even that of steel.

Suddenly there was a knife blade at the back of his neck.

A little boy, scratched and ragged, his face and hands dirty, dried tear-stains on his cheeks, had slit the tent-silk and entered unseen from the rear.

117

To the throat of the frozen Prince, whose wide green eyes mirrored his shock and surprise, he held the long poignard he had carried all the way from Zaradon.

Palensus Choy had guessed the knife might come in handy, when he had heard Kurdi had taken it. And he was so right!

14.

THE PROBLEM IN PARDOGA

Ganelon came awake very slowly, and in several distinct stages. Someone held a leather cup of cold, foamy beer to his lips and he gulped it down thirstily: it was delicious.

He felt singularly queer. His head was heavy, his brain seemed logy and congested, and his body was numb all over. He shook his head woozily to clear his wits, but it did little good. He peered about him with bleary, unfocused eyes, striving to ascertain his surroundings.

He was in a tent or pavilion of richly colored silk. Directly opposite him, a slim, delicate, nervous man in lordly raiment sat in a campaign chair, wetting thin lips with a pointed tongue and sweating profusely. Ganelon was certain that he had never set eyes on this personage before.

The last thing he could remember, he thought to himself sluggishly, was going to sleep in the forest. He had been in his own tent, a rough, nomadic thing of tanned hides—nothing like this dainty, silken pavilion.

Where was he? And, what was perhaps even more important, *what had happened here?*

Then, staring around him bewilderedly, he saw Kurdi standing behind the thin, nervous man who was dressed like a princeling, holding a dagger to his throat. And the world righted itself and came into focus.

"Kurdi! You're all right?" he demanded. "What's been happening here? Who is that man?"

The Prince cleared his throat—but carefully, mindful of the razor-edge of steel set lightly but unwaveringly against his throat—and attempted a smile of genial welcome which did not come off.

"*Hem!* You are in Pardoga, my dear fellow, and I am Prince Pergamon, the monarch of this realm and your, ah, your host. Do, please, have some more beer!"

The arousing of the Horde from their ensorceled slumbers was a slow and time-consuming task which occupied the Pardogamen the rest of that day and most of the evening, as well.

Prince Pergamon's knights attended to the job of overseeing the yeomen, and were themselves overseen by Ganelon Silvermane. Now much better, his head clear and his circulation restored, the Warlord had moved his chair out onto the meadow so as to keep an eye on the knights.

It had been agreed, as a reasonable precaution against any unpleasant incident, to disarm the Ximchak warriors before placing the amulets around their necks, thus breaking the enchantment under which they slept. Ganelon had agreed to this, knowing the quick temper of his men: wakening to find themselves surrounded by armed strangers, it would be an unusually cautious or easily intimidated Ximchak who would not grab his ax or sword or spear first and do a little bloodletting, asking questions later.

The Prince kept up a running commentary during this lengthy process, while the Champions were disenchanted first, then the Kuzaks, then the Warchiefs and chieftains of each tribe or Clan.

"Pardoga, you see, my dear fellow, was originally the domain of a powerful, and, if I *may* say so, rather cantankerous old magician. Of course, this was long before my ancestors led our people here when our own original homeland, Sorabdazon, was endangered by an incursion of Green Wraiths."

"Get to the point," growled Silvermane.

"Of course: quite right! Well, this magician fellow, you see, wanted his privacy. He prized it, I would say, above all else. The only open part of the borders of Pardoga—or what is *now* Pardoga, it had another name back then—was this part of the southeast, fronting upon the Uskodian Plain. So he caused the forest to grow: the Sleeping Forest, we call it, and for good reason, if I may say so!" the Prince giggled.

"And?"

"Well, you see, to the north the Pardogan border is rendered more or less impassable, by reason of the Fire Pits, and to the south we are walled in by one arm of the Rlambar Mountains, while, of course, to the *west*—to the *west*—well, I mean to say—!"

"About the forest?" Ganelon reminded him, trying to be patient.

"Yes; of course; well: this magician fellow, you understand, created the Sleeping Forest here, so as to block the only easily accessible entryway into his domain. The Forest, of course, is under an enchantment. A Sleeping Spell, I believe wizards call it. Any person, or bird or beast, or *whatever*, who strays across our border and enters the Forest very soon finds himself, or *her*self, or *it*self, well—*sleepy*."

"And, I gather, from that sleep he, her, or it never wakes up, is that it?" inquired Silvermane.

"That's the way of it, I'm very much afraid," the Prince confessed lamely. "Unless the spell is broken by the use of one of these protective talismans, that is. We have a couple of hundred of the amulets, as it happens. Bought them up in Lyzash, our neighbor to the north: City of Magicians up there, perhaps you've heard of it? Place called Warzoon? No finer place for thirty countries 'round, if you're in the market for talismans, periapts, amulets, fetishes, phylacteries, eidola, or charms."

"This magician—"

"Oh, long moved on, centuries ago! Fellow name of—let me see!—oh, yes, Uxorian Something-or-other—"

"Hrrm!" interrupted Sir Berglamum *sotto voce*. "Uxorian Maximus, Sire."

"Yes, of course: good fellow, Berglamum. Uxorian Maximus, that was his name," nodded Prince Pergamon.

Ganelon said nothing. As it happened, he had heard of this

Uxorian Maximus before. During his travels and adventures, he had encountered more than once an artifact or invention left behind by the famous magician. It had been this same Maximus, in fact, to whom the creation of the dangerous Indigon herds was generally attributed.

By late evening, the last of the Horde had been aroused from the enchanted sleep, and no one seemed the worse for the uncanny experience, save for about fifty of the older warriors who had succumbed without awakening.

The Ximchaks, however, awoke with ravenous appetites, having slept through breakfast, lunch, and dinner. Prince Pergamon, understandably anxious to avoid any unpleasantness, sent his two companies of knights out to scour the countryside to the north and west of the Forest for viands wherewith to feed his unexpected guests.

Herds, arbors, groves, farms, and fields for miles around were pressed for a levy of foodstuffs, and under the luminous immensity of the Falling Moon, an hour or two after midnight, an enormous and tasty, if rather hastily cobbled together, feast was spread for the grumbling, surly-tempered Ximchaks.

By the time the very last crumb, morsel, and drop of nutriment had vanished down the tens of thousands of Ximchak gullets, it was far too late for everyone to mount up and begin the trip north to Sargish, so tents were pitched to the west of the vast Sleeping Forest, sentries were mounted, and everybody turned in for a few hours of slumber until daybreak.

None of the Ximchaks felt very much like going to sleep again, in such near proximity to the enchanted tract of woodland, but there was nothing else for them to do to fill the nocturnal hours.

Prince Pergamon shared the hospitality of Ganelon's own tent, more as a hostage to ensure his knights would not seize the opportunity afforded by the darkness after moonset to attack the Barbarians, than for any other reason. A wary truce of sorts existed between the Ximchaks and the Pardogamen; but it was perfectly obvious that the knights of the Green Banneret and the Red Lance would prefer to be rid of the Ximchak army, if not by one means then by another.

Still and all, they were outnumbered hundreds to one, and

a surprise attack was very unlikely. Keeping the Prince of Pardoga in their midst, however, was some additional insurance.

With dawn they woke, struck their tents, assembled their beasts, loaded up the wains, and headed north for the capital. It took three days to reach the fertile plain in whose midst the city of Sargish arose, at the junction of the two rivers of Thash and Ubbolon.

For the next ten days the Horde lay encamped before Sargish, lavishly feasting off the involuntary hospitality of the Pardogamen. Ganelon thought it was the least Prince Pergamon could do: he was well aware that, had it not been for little Kurdi and his long knife, the sardonic monarch would have stripped the warriors of the Horde of their every last possession while they slept the sleep of death, and buried them callously once life had departed.

The Clan Warchiefs argued that the thing to do was to fall upon Sargish and level it to the ground, exterminating the knights and plundering the ruins. This, they pointed out, was the good, old-fashioned Ximchak way, hallowed by tradition.

Ganelon explained that he was unable to do that, for he was honor-bound by the promise Kurdi had made.

In return for the lives of the Horde warriors, the boy had been forced to promise that the Ximchaks would assist in the final solution of the problem that had long vexed the people of Pardoga.

And that problem was the Strange Little Men of the Hills.

The leaders of the Horde shrugged at this: to their way of thinking, a promise extorted under a threat could safely be forgotten, once the threat was past. And the Horde *really wanted* to loot, plunder, burn, and ravage Sargish; it was the sort of thing they did best: also, they hadn't had a crack at any looting, plundering, burning or ravaging since Gompery, at least.

To which Ganelon replied that the disenchantment of the Horde had been extorted from Prince Pergamon under the threat of Kurdi's knife. The Prince had made good his side of the bargain: could the Ximchaks do any less than to fulfill their own half of the deal?

While they were chewing that one over, he added a final

argument: the only way out of Pardoga—unless they went back by the same way they had come in, and that was called "retreating"—was to the west.

Which meant they were going to have to confront the Strange Little Men of the Hills anyway. They might as well do so with their honor intact, by fulfilling their half of the bargain by which Kurdi had bartered for their lives.

There was a lot of grumbling, grousing, griping, and grexing, but in the end it was agreed.

The following hot summer day Ganelon rode into Sargish to confer with Prince Pergamon and his advisers concerning the problem of the Strange Little Men of the Hills.

He was guarded by his Champions, of course, plus a full company of Kuzaks. Kurdi, Grrff the Xombolian, and Ishgadara the Gynosphinx went with him. So did the War-chiefs of the Nine Clans.

There was no reason to fear treachery or betrayal on the part of the Pardogamen. For, in case the leaders of the Horde were poisoned or cut down or imprisoned, the Ximchaks would attack the city anyway. Ganelon politely made certain that Prince Pergamon understood this fact clearly, in advance.

The royal palace of Sargish was a tall, towering affair of many slender spires, roofed with blue glass which permitted the sunlight to bathe the upper chambers in a superb azure luminance. Although Sargish, and the rest of Pardoga, for that matter, was going to be hungry for months, its granaries and storehouses rapidly being emptied in order to feed the tens of thousands of unexpected guests camping on their very doorstep, the palace corps of chefs managed to scrape together a hearty lunch for the visitors.

Over the traditional Pardogan after-dinner drink (beer), they got down to cases.

The problem in Pardoga was, quite simply, the Strange Little Men.

No one knew who or what they were.

Nor where they had come from, nor exactly when.

They infested the Dark Hills directly opposite the plain in the midst of which the city of Sargish was situated. These hills, which were low and easily passable (under ordinary circumstances, anyway), constituted the western border of Pardoga.

The way west was the one easily traveled route out of Pardoga. Or, for all of that, *into* Pardoga.

The other borders of Pardoga were blocked by one or another kind of natural barrier, which made travel to and fro hazardous, costly, and time-consuming.

The way west was blocked by a most *unnatural* barrier: the Strange Little Men.

What was so strange about them was that hardly anyone had ever actually seen them and returned to tell of it.

And those that had did not seem to describe them in the same way as earlier survivors.

Some said they were tall and skinny and long-legged, covered with a slick white integument, like Youks. Others said they were short and stump-legged, colored a vile, poison green, like Death Dwarves. Still others reported them flying or floating disembodied crania, like the Talking Heads of Soorm. There were even a few who bore back descriptions of them as wispy, vaporish creatures, not unlike the Green Wraiths.

The one thing everyone agreed upon was that they were very deadly. Travelers, merchants, military expeditions, pilgrims, wandering knights and troubadours, even outlaw bands and companies of brigands—they slew them all, leaving no survivors.

Or very few survivors, at any rate.

Prince Pergamon had sent squads and then companies, followed in time by entire regiments and even heavy brigades to clear them out of the hills. They had vanished without a trace.

His father, Prince Periander, and *his* father before him, Prince Pluridus, had done the same thing, with the same result.

The Strange Little Men never came out of their hills to bother the people of Pardoga, or at least they had never done so in recorded history.

But they *might*. There was certainly nothing to prevent them from doing so. And the very existence of that possibility was a living nightmare to the Pardogamen.

They had lived under the shadow of that nameless and

threatening, that mysterious horror which hovered on their border, for so very long that they would do anything to rid themselves of it.

The Warchiefs of the Horde could see no reason why they should be stopped by Strange Little Men or anything else.

No matter how strong these uncanny creatures were, or how numerous or cunning or dangerous, the mighty Ximchaks, in their warlike and unconquerable thousands, were surely stronger, more numerous, just as cunning, and every bit as dangerous.

They had crushed empires, shattered kingdoms, whelmed ⹂d trampled underfoot realms and regions ere now. A ⹂mple, ordinary stretch of hills—Strange Little Men or *no* Strange Little Men—was not going to slow them down, much ⹂ss stop them in their tracks.

Such, at least, was the bluff and bluster of the Warchiefs.

Ganelon did not feel quite so confident.

It seemed to him, from what he had seen of them, that the mailed and mounted knights of Pardoga were a hardy legion of fighting men, well disciplined, brave enough, veteran war-riors all. Still, they lacked the berserker qualities of his Ximchaks, their fighting fury, their sheer, overpowering weight of numbers.

So he agreed to let them try.

Over the next three days, the Horde broke camp and marched west across the plains, to set up new encampments in a wide half-circle, facing the Dark Hills.

A tribe of Urziki vied for the honor of entering the hill country. Ganelon gravely gave his consent.

Five hundred strong, mounted on fleet-footed orniths, heavily armed and wary, they rode into the hills, and not a single one of them came back.

Two days later, Ganelon gave his permission for a triple assault to be made. At three different points along the edge of the hills, each assault point about five miles due south of the other, heavy squadrons of Gurzimen, Hoys, and Tharradians rode into the darkness between the hills, some twelve hundred fifty Ximchaks in all.

None of them came back, either.

Nor was there any sound of battle that came echoing

through the stillness of the morning. It was as if twelve hundred alert and ready warriors had ridden into nothingness, and had dispersed into vapor.

Lord Saphur, Warchief of the Qarrs, and Ovvo Redtooth of the Farthamen, both begged permission of the Warlord to lead expeditions a thousand strong against the Strange Little Men.

Ganelon refused.

The Horde was vast, and incomparably strong; but no army is so mighty that it can shrug off the loss of seventeen hundred and fifty men, then gamble away the lives of two thousand more. The Horde was already seriously understrength, he pointed out: ill-advised expeditions into the south had cost the army a total of fourteen thousand, three hundred men before Valardus, at Mount Naroob, at the Bryza, and on the Ovarva Plains. Now the count of the dead was swollen by the seventeen hundred and fifty they had recently lost to the Strange Little Men. Not to mention the two hundred old and sick warriors who had died the winter just past in Gompery, and the fifty men who had not waked from the spell of the Sleeping Forest.

Ovvo Redtooth and Lord Saphur were adamant, however, and they finally prevailed again over his innate sense of prudence. He warned them to observe every precaution, to send out scouts and outriders, and to retreat at the first sign of anything queer.

They agreed.

Next morning, two thousand strong, Farthamen and Qarrs rode into the Dark Hills.

And never came back.

15.

THE STRANGE LITTLE MEN OF THE HILLS

Ganelon sat in the stifling midsummer evening heat of his tent, gloomily contemplating a bleak future. Four days ago, he had, very much against his wishes, permitted two thousand Qarrs and Farthamen to ride to their doom, and with them had gone two of the great Warchiefs.

It was now twenty-seven days since they had left the Petrified City of Ruxor, and about three months since they turned west at Pathon Thad. It was four months and eight days since he had led the great Ximchak Horde out of Gompia through the Vigola Pass.

In those four months and eight days they had journeyed many hundreds of miles into the west, without fighting a single battle or suffering even one attack.

And he had lost thirty-seven hundred men. No, three thousand seven hundred and fifty, counting those who had not reawakened from the enchantment of the Sleeping Forest.

It was enough to plunge any Warlord into a gloomy and melancholic mood.

To make things worse, the Horde was clamoring for action.

Men had been lost from the Clans of Urzik, Gurzi, Hoy, Tharrad, Qarr and Fartha.

Their comrades of the Gurko, Rooxa and Kazool Clans were ferociously demanding a chance at avenging the lost warriors. They boasted they could outfight the other Clans with one hand tied behind them, and were clamoring for permission to prove it.

If things weren't already bad enough, two of the Clans were now leaderless, and their various tribal chieftains were trying to outmaneuver each other for promotion to the War-chieftaincies left vacant by the mysterious deaths of Ovvo Redtooth and Lord Saphur. A dozen tribal chiefs and subchiefs had died already from poison, duels, or knives in the back.

The entire Horde was splitting into rival factions. Unless something was done, and quickly, the Nine Clans would be at each other's throats, and open rioting and pitched battles would rip the Horde asunder.

If that happened, probably the knightly companies of Pardoga would attack, if only on the pretext of protecting Sargish.

Ganelon was smack in the middle of the most serious test he had yet faced since he had become Warlord of the Horde six and a half months before.

And he knew it.

But what was there to do? Lead the entire Horde into the Dark Hills? To do that probably meant the entire Horde would suffer the same mysterious fate as the thirty-seven hundred lost warriors. Retreat from the hills? The morale in the Horde was already sour enough: to retreat would be to admit he was defeated. He would probably lose the Warlordship if he tried to turn back now.

Oddly enough, it was Ishgadara who provided him with the suggestion of a solution to his problem.

The big, cheerful sphinx-girl seldom volunteered ideas or suggestions of her own: she was content to merely go along with what the others decided. But she was far from being unintelligent, was Ishgadara, and in this case her quick wits came up with a shrewd answer to the question which had been plaguing Ganelon.

"Why you no sendingk soldiers through, while Ishy

watchum from offerhead?" she inquired helpfully. "Then me can see what happen to um."

Ganelon gawped at her, thunderstruck by the simplicity of the idea. Why had so obvious a solution to the mystery not occurred to him? His old master, the Illusionist, had always warned him to use his wits, to think his way out of problems, rather than to rely on his great strength. *There will come a time when strength and even courage avail you nothing, m'boy,* the Illusionist had cautioned him once. *Then you will wish you had learned to use your head!*

"Ishy, you're a genius!" he enthused, wrapping his arms about the Gynosphinx and hugging her fondly.

"Sure," she grinned, wagging her lion's tail. "Pretty, too!"

The next day he called for volunteers: hundreds of Ximchaks responded, but from them he chose only twenty-five, all older warriors without families, and many of them sick or lame or injured.

Mounted on the broad back of the sphinx-girl, he and Grrff soared into the morning sky. Below, at a prearranged signal, the volunteer force cautiously entered the hills.

For a time the old warriors trudged along the dusty road which wound between hills and hummocks of spongy gray soil, dry and crumbling, while Ishgadara soared above their heads on her strong bronze wings.

"There's something," growled Grrff. Then, blinking incredulously, he said: "My claws an' whiskers—what *is* that thing?"

Ganelon stared, eyes watering in the brisk wind of Ishy's beating wings.

Below them, on the knoll of a low hummock overlooking the winding road, a small hunched figure had suddenly appeared. It was seated tailor-fashion, looking down unconcernedly upon the approaching Ximchaks. It seemed unaware of the flying creature overhead in the sky.

It wore the likeness of a diminutive, hunched, gnomelike little old man with an enormous proboscis of a nose. It seemed naked: its wizened, scrawny body black and glittering, like anthracite coal. For eyes it had dim red glitters under an overhanging brow, like dull chip-rubies. Besides the eyes, and the huge nose, they could discern no other features.

The little creature carried no weapons, and looked too

small and frail and harmless to possibly afford any threat or danger to the alert, seasoned warriors trooping up the road between the gray hills.

As they came directly beneath it, the black gnome suddenly thrust out one arm in a stiff gesture.

Then things happened almost too swiftly for the eye of those flying above to discern:

The black stick-thin arm *melted away* into swirling vapor.

A boiling, writhing haze of sparkling black granules whipped around the marching warriors.

Suddenly, the mist of mineral dust vanished—and the warriors were coated with black powder!

Frozen stiff, they tottered and fell, some of them. Others stood motionless, like statues cut from black stone.

"Great Gal-*en*-dil!" breathed Ganelon. "Down, girl, quick! Before they smother!"

Ishgadara tilted sharply, and slid down in a tight spiral.

"Look out!" roared the Tigerman, hackles rising along his spine. "More of the black devils!"

Ganelon blinked against the rushing wind. Six or seven more black gnomes had materialized on the crest of nearer hills. They looked up, regarding the rapidly descending Gynosphinx and her riders blandly, without consternation.

One lazily extended an arm in the same stiff, jerky motion as the first. The arm vanished to the elbow in a whiff of black, whirling powder which speared into the air directly for them. Ishgadara veered to one side, dodging the seemingly innocent plume of black dust.

"My fangs an' fur! Look there—"

Ganelon followed Grrff's pointing paw and saw an astonishing sight. The dry gray soil of the hill bases was churning and boiling like thick lava. Out of the soft earth fifty or sixty of the hunched black gnomes popped into view. They seized the motionless black-coated figures of the conquered Ximchaks and began to drag them back into the surface of the hills.

As they did so, the black dust suddenly detached itself from the men, who were dead of asphyxiation by this time, most likely. Like a swarm of diminutive, sentient black gnats, the glittering granules rose from the limp bodies, whirled into the air, and reshaped into the missing arm of the first gnome.

Ishgadara swung down to the lower level again, but it was too late. The toiling gnomes had dragged the corpses back into the hills, the crumbling soil closed behind them, forming a smooth wall again. One by one the gnomes squatting atop the knolls popped back underground. They dove in nose first, Ganelon noticed with awe, and the soft soil opened to receive them.

Ishgadara regained the upper air, circled about, and headed back for camp. Grrff tried not to notice that Ganelon was weeping.

After all, he had just sent twenty-five men to their deaths, and had been unable to save them. He had a right to weep, had Ganelon Silvermane.

That the Strange Little Men of the Hills were a new form of sentient mineral life was by now obvious.

Such phenomena were not unknown on Gondwane in this far age. According to the theorists, all forms of matter evolve continuously toward the goal of life, even of intelligence. The intellectual crystalloids found around Oth-Yom-Barqa, the Stone Heads of Soorm—such things were not entirely unknown, although certainly rare.

Apparently, the Strange Little Men were solid structures of black crystal, able to disperse and control their component particles. The Ximchaks, suddenly locked in sheaths of living mineral, were helpless to move or struggle. The dust, blocking their nostrils, had smothered them.

The Little Men were tougher and denser than the dry soil of the Hills, able to come and go through the solid earth with less difficulty than men find wading through deep water. They had no need to breath, requiring no oxygen for combustion, although the mode and manner of their nutrition, and how they sustained their life processes, remained unguessable.

The mystery of how they had, so swiftly and with such little fuss or bother, managed to overwhelm and dispose of thousands of vigilant, heavily armed warriors, was solved.

But the problem remained.

How do you fight something made of pure mineral, much less kill the thing?

"It's like fighting magic," Ganelon confessed a day or two

later, having exhausted his wits against the stubborn problem. "Strength alone is no good: you need *better* magic."

Luckily he knew a powerful magician. . . .

The next morning Ishgadara and Grrff departed on an important mission.

Three days later, the Flying Castle of Zaradon appeared in the skies above the encampment of the Horde, and settled to a landing amidst the Plains.

The skinny, absent-minded magician Palensus Choy, and his friend Ollub Vetch, the fat little inventor, greeted Ganelon effusively. They were delighted to see their erstwhile companion once again, pleased at the ingenious manner in which he had removed the Ximchak problem out of Gompery and away from the countries of Greater Zuavia, and more than willing to help him and his warriors against the Strange Little Men of the Hills.

The Ximchaks had been very unhappy at the arrival of the fantastic Flying Castle. The aerial edifice had crushed thousands upon thousands of their brethren at Mount Naroob and on the Ovarva Plains, and the memory of that tremendous defeat and its resultant slaughter still rankled within them.

"It has never been the way of the Ximchaks to become friendly with former enemies," said Lord Barzik sternly, when Ganelon had first presented his plan before the Council.

"I told you months ago that, to survive, you must be more adaptable," Ganelon said firmly. "The Ximchaks must change their ways, if they would live."

"I still don't like the idea," grumbled the Gurko Warchief.

"Would you rather I sent the entire Horde marching into the Hills?" demanded Silvermane in a stern voice. "A few thousand might come through: we would only lose one hundred and fifty thousand men, if we were lucky."

Even Lord Barzik had no answer to that one. So Palensus Choy came.

With him were Grrff the Xombolian and Ishgadara. The sphinx-girl was happy to return in the Flying Castle, rather than do all the flying herself. Ganelon discussed the problem with the two savants. When he was finished, the magician combed his long wispy beard thoughtfully, peering absently into the middle distance.

133

"Rather difficult problem, I should say. For all my sorcery, I can't call to mind an easy solution thereto. Sentient forms of mineral life partake of the elemental strength of Old Earth herself, and are remarkably resistant to sorcery."

"Science, then, hey? *That's* the thing you need, ye need, lad!" puffed the fat inventor eagerly. Ganelon tried not to grin: Palensus Choy and Ollub Vetch, apparently, still had not resolved their long-running feud as to the relative superiority of science or sorcery.

"Perhaps you're right," he mused. Suddenly there flashed into his mind something that had happened about one year and three months ago, when the Red Enchantress had attacked the Mobile City of Kan Zar Kan. The City had englobed the Witch Queen in a sphere of imperishable plastic, hurling her into the hyperspatial tube. For all he knew, she was still imprisoned by this means; according to the City, the synthetic crystal was indestructible, proof alike to the forces of nature and the powers of magic.

On impulse, Ganelon related this incident to his friends. They were interested, Vetch in particular, and decided to look into the matter at once. The secret of the synthetic crystal might indeed be the solution to their problem.

The next morning, Zaradon departed on a long flight into the southeast, flying over the two Arzenias, and the lower tip of Greater Zuavia, bound for the Purple Plains. Somewhere in that vast waste of lavender grasses, Kan Zar Kan was currently situated. King Yemple would certainly welcome the visitors with Iomagothic hospitality, they being old friends.

And Ganelon sat down grimly to wait and see.

The days passed slowly. Forage parties went out from the camp at intervals, bringing back game and cattle. The rivers were almost depleted of fish, and other supplies of edibles were nearly exhausted.

If something didn't happen soon, the Horde must either begin to starve, or attack Sargish and seize its granaries.

Ten days dragged slowly by in this manner. Then, quite suddenly one early evening about sundown, the Flying Castle appeared in the skies over the Dark Hills.

Floating against a sky of tangerine flame, the aerial edifice extruded, by some unguessed orifice, an immense, shimmering bubble.

Glimmering with evanescent hues, like a hollow moon of lambent opal, the wobbling sphere expanded until it was miles across.

Then it detached itself from the Castle, and drifted downward.

The instant it touched the crest of the hills, it vanished. Now the hills glistened in the rich flame of sunset as if heavily sheathed in gleaming frost.

From a spire, the Palace emitted an intense flash of spluttering green light. Brilliant as a falling star, piercing the gloom, the green ray flickered intermittently, bathing the glass-sheathed hills in fierce emerald luminance.

The light vanished. Zaradon waggled from side to side, as if in salute, and ascended, returning to Mount Naroob.

And that was all there was to it.

At dawn the next morning, the Horde broke camp and began to march the hills.

The clawed feet of the orniths and the heavy, lumbering nguamadons squeaked and slipped on the glassy stuff, but the Ximchaks drove their beasts on.

The hills were armored now in tough, unbreakable plastic of a manufacture known only to Kan Zar Kan and Palensus Choy—or was it Ollub Vetch?

For tens of square miles the hills and the roads and ways between them were thickly sheathed in the glittering, glassy stuff.

Traversing the hills, the Ximchaks laughed at the antics of the furious gnomes. They flailed behind the glass walls of their transparent prison, scratching with black claws, pecking with their beaklike noses, churning the soft earth into mush as they threshed and scrabbled.

But nothing they could do would ever penetrate the unbreakable lucency wherewith the Flying Castle of Zaradon had sprayed the Hills of the Strange Little Men.

The Horde passed on, into Shu and Chemba.

Book Four
THE MERDINGIAN REGNATE

The Scene: Upper Arzenia: The Marvelous Mountains; Malme River Country; the Empty Cities; Urd, Spoyda, and other Merdingian Cities.

New Characters: Droga Oneeye and Niamba the Farthaman; King Yottle and other Voygych River Brigands; the Five Peers of Merdingia.

16.

BEYOND THE MARVELOUS MOUNTAINS

Particularly in the dark-red sunsets peculiar to this region bordering the Malme River Country, the mountainous vista was spectacular, thought Ganelon Silvermane.

The night air was crisp and keen, the season being mid-fall. He drew his cloak of furs more closely about his naked torso, lingering for one last look of the mountains in the wine-red light, before it failed. He would come out again later, to view the Marvelous Mountains by the radiance of the Falling Moon.

They were aptly named, these mountains. Nothing in all of those regions of Gondwane known to him could compare to this stupendous spectacle. Perhaps the famous Carven Cliffs down in Uchamboy, far, far to the south, bore some similarity to the Marvelous Mountains, but he had only heard tell of that wonder.

Who had sculpted this entire range of purple mountains into fantastic seated figures, throned colossi, fabulous monsters, frowning faces, no one could say for certain. According to Selestor's *Geography*, it had been a long-extinct race called the Artisans of Zed, an obscure civilization obsessed by thoughts of mortality, who were thought to have devoted the entire energies of their race to the construction of immense, incredible monuments which they hoped would endure even the death of the sun, and bear eternal testimony to the fact of their existence. To these Artisans of Zed were attributed such spectacular achievements as the Yeshian Wall, the Amber Ziggurat in Palambar, and the hundred-mile-long Earth Paintings in High Hroach. Commentaries on Selestor, however, considered the attribution of the Marvelous Mountains to the monomaniacal Zed builders as dubious, since they were never known to stray from the regions peculiar to them.

The entire mountain range was of pure lapis lazuli, which was marvelous enough: the glittering purple mineral, however, streaked through with rich indigo and paling, here and there, to striations of milky azure, had been worked with unimaginable effort into a titanic thousand-mile frieze of figures, groupings, enormous visages, and weird beasts. The third range, directly below him, bore, for example, the likenesses, scrupulously accurate according to the opinions of zoologists, of the thirty-seven known varieties of gargoyle. And, opposite him, nine peaks of soaring heights, all of equal altitude, had been graven into portraits of the divinities of the Maldane Mythos; only the likenesses of Orcys, Pargetta, Lady Lionore, Ardix the Grim, Father Hu, and Dio and Dia, the Heavenly Twins, could today be recognized, although the two remaining peaks, both partially demolished by the Meteor Rains of the previous Eon, had once borne recognizable features of Granos and Jeraine, if the tales of ancient travelers were veritable.

The vinous light had darkened now to lavender; the titanic faces and robed forms now were obliviated by shadows. From the flap of the tent behind him there wafted on the evening breezes the delicious odors of stewed succulents, yikyik cutlets, and jungleberry soup.

Ganelon went in to dinner.

It had taken the Horde two weeks and a day to cross Shu and Chemba, and they had lingered four days in Quoyd, the Sacerdotal City, to enjoy the triannual Immolations.

The losses they had suffered in vain expeditions against the Strange Little Men of the Hills had somewhat soured their appetite for warfare, evidently, for no one suggested to the

Warlord that they should sack Quoyd, or even attack it.

The famous poverty of the Sacerdotal City might, in part, account for the Ximchaks' most un-Barbarian reluctance to lay siege to the holy metropolis. Or, it might well be, they remembered all too well the unique and curious doom which had befallen Wazary the Ferocious after he led his Red Clans against the priests' city.*

The mild, zestful weather of late summer (unusually comfortable for these lowlands) had perhaps awakened their dormant fondness for loot, plunder, and rapine. For they spent the ensuing twenty-one days in a vain and costly attack against the Triple City of Hylage, Janeel and Corascio. More than two hundred lives were lost in an attempt to scale the Glass Walls which surrounded the Triple City, and another five hundred were wasted in wall-top battle against the packs of trained and hungry yaglarks maintained by the Tripolitarians atop the broad barrier for precisely that reason, the discouragement of unwelcome visitors.

Ganelon had warned them that the Triple City was too ably protected, but they had outvoted him in Council. After three weeks, they slunk from Hylage, Janeel and Corascio, with bitter curses and depleted ranks.

During the ten days it took the Horde to pass through the Narrow Vale which led between the towering ramp heights of the dangerous Warbird Cliffs, they had suffered the loss of more than two hundred and fifty more warriors to death or cripplement. This route had been selected as potentially less dangerous than the Maroon Swamps to the south or the slippery, treacherous surfaces of Irimouth Glacier to the north.

The Warbirds who infested the sheer cliffs, nesting in the innumerable caves, clefts and crevices, were a larger and more rapacious variety of the patrol-hawks they had seen in Pardoga, their sheening plumage so intensely blue as to be almost jet in normal light, where the hawks had gone sheathed in feathers of metallic azure.

For considerable portions of the year, the Warbirds toler-

---

* While the text of the Epic does not expand upon this cryptic reference, the Ninth Commentary explains that the Red Clan conqueror was seized by an uncontrollable passion for serpents and was crushed in the coils of a monstrous sky serpent atop Mount Arish, while attempting to satisfy his unnatural lust.

ated trespassers through the vale, but this, unfortunately, had proved their nesting season, and the parent birds were testy, argumentative, and, I'm afraid, quite ravenous. Ganelon felt lucky to have brought his troops through with no more losses than had been suffered.

For three days they circled around Elfry, unwilling to risk the ire of its resident god, Ioh, reputed to be thirty feet in height, six-armed, and invulnerable to anything save water.

More recently, they had loitered their way for the last six days, traveling through the Marvelous Mountains and gawping at the magnificent views and vistas.

It was nearly two months since they had passed out of Pardoga—fifty-nine days, to be exact—and fall was nearly done. Ganelon planned to lead them south, into the Merdingian Regnate, before winter came down upon the world.

He did not expect any trouble on the way.

The Horde had recovered much of its morale and sense of unity, although its defeat at the Triple City and the harrowing, bloody trip between the Warbird Cliffs had given it little to feel proud of, recently.

Ganelon had put a stop to the intertribal feuds in the two leaderless Clans, which had wasted the lives of forty or so men, and oversaw the election of Droga Oneeye to the Warchieftaincy of the Qarrs, filling the vacancy left by Lord Saphur when he and his regiment perished in the expedition against the Strange Little Men. Niamba of the Farthamen, in a like manner, assumed the leadership of his Clan: as tenth and youngest son of Ovvo Redtooth, he was the obvious choice—especially since his nine older brothers had died in the feuds.

In this way, peace was restored. For a while, anyway.

There was still the problem of Ruzara, of course.

The former Gompish princess, wearying of throwing herself at Ganelon Silvermane, sulked and wept and pouted for a time, as any woman would do when scorned (however gently and politely) by the man for whom she has conceived a searing passion.

But a woman as young and beautiful as Ruzara of Gompery does not go long without suitors. Ganelon, hoping to cure her of her infatuation for him, saw to it that bold, handsome, gay young Harsha of the Horn was brought into close proximity with the unhappy girl on every conceivable occasion.

This was at the advice of Grrff. The Tigerman was no stranger to the tender passion, and had left ten or was it twelve litters of cubs back in Karjixia, when he began his travels. Thus he knew considerably more about the female heart than the innocent Silvermane.

" 'Course, we Tigermen don't mate fer life, you know," he confided on the evening of first advising Silvermane to throw Ruzara and the gallant and vigorous Herald together. "Once or twice a year, our females go into heat, and we sorta pair off with 'em, if y' know what ol' Grrff means," he grinned, giving the blank, uncomprehending Warlord a meaningful nudge in the ribs with his furry elbow.

Alas, such was the innocence of Ganelon Silvermane that the poor fellow actually *didn't* know, and Grrff's suggestive winks and leers left him as ignorant as before. Oh, I suppose Silvermane knew *intellectually*, more or less, what the Tigerman meant—he knew that to make babies (or, in Karjixian terms, cubs), the mother and the father ... well, did It together.

But exactly what It was, Ganelon really didn't know. And was too polite, or too gentlemanly, or both, to come right out and *ask*.

Besides which, he wasn't honestly interested.

But he figured Grrff *must* know what he was talking about. After all, there were all those litters of cubs, whose existence would otherwise have been unaccountable. So he accepted the suggestion of the Tigerman, and assigned Harsha of the Horn to ride with Ruzara henceforth.

That Harsha had long been enamoured of the girl from Gompland was old news to the Ximchaks. That he had, thus far, succeeded in gaining nothing other than her scorn was equally familiar knowledge to the warriors.

They took bets on whether or not Harsha's gay, laughing ways, romantic seranades, and covert wooing would bear fruit. Or whether the forlorn, heartsick, and headstrong girl would do something foolish, like trying to drug Ganelon with a love philtre, or sneak into his tent at nightfall, or something equally desperate.

They didn't know it, the wagering Ximchaks, but the answer to these questions was only days away.

Over the next four days, the Horde continued to troop through that awesome and spectacular extravagance of gleaming purple lapis, the Marvelous Mountains.

Down through the foothills they traveled, entering Malme River Country, a broad plain watered by innumerable small streams which meandered lazily between groves of bard trees and fields of chartreuse grasses ablaze with patches of star-flower.

By night the air was lively with the humming songs of the bard trees, whose stiff, branching, flexive and leafless fronds played the wind like harpstrings.

And the meadows flashed and dazzled as if they were treading the night skies underfoot, lit by the erratic phos-phorescent glows and gleams and glimmers of the luminous flowers, that twinkled and flickered and shone like the stars after which they were named.

By day they passed the Empty Cities. Once these aban-doned metropoli had been the homes of the Malmanian Dy-nasts, a race of blue men with peculiar white eyes remotely akin to the Witches of distant Yombok. Here they had dwelt for countless generations, before packing up and moving on in disgust. It was said of the Malmanians that they had been a proud people, vain of the splendor of their cities, unable to endure for very long living within sight of the Marvelous Mountains, whose sensational sculpture gave them an inferi-ority complex. Hence, finding the proximity to the carven peaks unendurable, they departed one night, wandering north, to found a new nation beyond Zarge.

The Empty Cities, however, as the Ximchaks found after seven days of journeying deep into the River Country, were no longer empty.

Broadest of the hundred rivers of the Malme Country was the Phrene. At the juncture of that river and the Nixie Hills was a place marked on the charts as Hilford: here it was that the Ximchaks attempted to ford the level, silvery floods of the placid Phrene.

It was the evening of their seventh day in the River Country. Night had fallen, thick and dense with fogs. Under the cover of the moonless dark, their swift, light, wedge-shaped attack barges hidden in the wreathing mists, the River Brigands suddenly struck.

Before the Ximchaks knew it, they were in the middle of a hot, fast, furious battle.

The Brigands had eyes that burned through the murk like the eyes of cats, slitted orbs of green phosphor. They were burly and swarthy of skin, with strangely short legs and curiously elongated arms, which lent them an appearance of, if not deformity, then at least unfinishedness.

Their heads were bald, whether naturally hairless or carefully shaven no one could say, and atop their pates they wore small, round, scarlet skullcaps like yarmulkes. (These later proved to be only painted on.)

The most alarming thing about them was that they had no noses, nor even nostril slits: to permit the intake of valued oxygen, still a basic requirement for most all forms of life even in this remote era whereof I tell, they perforce breathed through their mouths, held always open for that essential purpose.

They were disgusting in yet other ways I will not go into here, as mine is a family publisher.

The River Brigands were sprung from a people called the Voygych, a savage race of noseless nomads who, being unable to erect any of the monuments of civilization on their own, had adopted a quaint life-style. They moved into abandoned cities, empty towns, ruined structures of antiquity, or whatever, always pretending they were themselves the authors of these edifices. Their posturing fooled nobody, but they were too stupid, or too insensitive, to realize this. Probably, they were both.

They lived by a combination of brigandage, piracy, waylaying, robbery, ambushing, thievery, and the collection of taxes. (There have always been such people in every age, especially as regards the collecting of taxes.) Right now, it was brigandage.

At the moment they were resident in the Empty Cities of Kajja, Lemmery, and Serrium, while Uroph, to the north, held the larger part of them. Tireless copulators, it being their only sport, art, science, or recreation, they spawned immense families.

They were terrific fighters, given to squalling, furious rages, and battling without the least thought of injury, caution, prudence, or tactics. But, on the whole, and in the best of times, they were by nature a timid and unaggressive people, whose notion of daring was to murder innocent travelers from ambush, or to hold up and rob merchant caravans traveling through the mountains, under threat of Voygych-triggered avalanches.

Their king was an immense fat monarch, given to lechery, gluttony, torture, and cheap wine, called Yottle. He held in terrified superstitious veneration the great Glassfish who inhabited the streams, lakes, rivers, pools, canals, and ponds of Malme. One of these, a centuries-old specimen grown huge enough to swallow men whole, King Yottle considered the avatar of his tribal god Glugluck. Those among the Voygych unlucky enough to incur the enmity, ire, wrath, or jealousy of Yottle were usually fed alive to the finny incarnation of Glugluck. (Invariably, they drowned, as Glugluck, or at least the monstrous Glassfish who bore that name, by his nature fed on algae alone. The condemned Voygych, however, were tossed into Lake Parge trussed hand and foot, so there were seldom survivors.)

The Battle of the Phrene was over in about fifteen minutes, but during that brief span some seventy-five Ximchaks perished, either drowning (Ximchaks make poor swimmers under the best of circumstances) or falling to the darts of the Brigands.

Before the Ximchaks could rally enough to attack themselves, the Voygych barges were off downriver. Made of balsa-light wood laminated in heavy oil, the mobile craft were swift, surprisingly maneuverable, and sturdy.

Ganelon was nonplussed. He would have sent his Kuzaks after the hit-and-run Voygych Brigands, but they were stationed behind the Horde, protecting its rear. And his personal guard, the Champions, he had scattered throughout the host, controlling its movement for the fording.

It was the Gurkoes who had been hit, and Lord Barzik was furious over the ignominious way in which the Brigands had ripped them apart. True, they had been gingerly crossing in single file, each man mounted on his ornith, and the ornith, as oft as not, having to do as much swimming as walking, since the ford was none too shallow here. But still, a defeat is a defeat.

So Silvermane gave permission for Barzik and Harukh Irongrim to lead three hundred Gurkoes downstream in an attempt to catch the Rivermen. They rode off in haste, taking both sides of the Phrene.

Silvermane then conducted the rest of the Gurkoes across under guard, followed by interminable numbers of the Hoy.

Twice again during that endless night the Voygych Brigands made swift, devastating attacks by barge, both times hitting the Hoys, slaying about one hundred men in all.

The Ximchaks were furious.

By early morning the Gurkoes returned, what was left of them. The river, it seemed, had not narrowed, so that even when they got within sight of the Brigands, the Clansmen could do little. Their arrows inflicted only slight casualties among the hooting, grinning, sniggering Voygych, who sat there in the middle of the river and killed Gurko after Gurko after Gurko with shrewdly shot darts, at the use of which they were uncannily accurate, due either to their unusually long arms, or the fact that they could see very well in the dark.

Only one hundred and twenty Gurkoes rode back to Hilford, bearing their dead: they were bone-weary, dispirited, heads hanging.

Among the slain Ganelon was horrified to discover were Harukh Irongrim and Lord Barzik, the Gurko Warchief. The two old warriors had been the staunchest and most loyal of his supporters, and among his best friends in the Horde.

And now they were dead, at the hands of a dirty, ignorant crew of slovenly water pirates.

Ganelon set his jaw grimly. He did not like war, and had held the Ximchaks back from warfare wherever possible.

But now he was determined to eliminate these abominable Brigands to the last, miserable wretch of a Voygych.

Only later, when the count was made, was another casualty discovered. Ruzara was missing!

17.

THE RESCUING OF RUZARA

The Gompish girl, it seemed, had ridden deeply into the shallows, stung to fury by the killing of Lord Barzik. The rushing currents of the Phrene, swifter here than upriver, had dragged her from the saddle of her ornith, and the gleeful Brigands had hauled her, spluttering and half-drowned, into one of their barges.

She was the first captive the Voygych had taken from amongst the Horde, and no one knew exactly why they had captured her, rather than slaying her out of hand. However, Ganelon had a good idea why. Ruzara was extraordinarily beautiful.

Once the entire Horde was on the other side of Hilford, the Warlord assembled them into battle formation, and hurled them against the nearer of the Empty Cities, a place marked as Kajja on the charts. It was clearly occupied, as the smoke of cooking fires could be seen rising in the morning air, and more than a few of the Voygych clustered upon the walls, observing the advance of the Ximchaks.

No one knew just how long the city had lain empty and abandoned by its builders before being taken over by the wandering Voygych bands, but the walls, at least, were in good repair. Against those towering stone ramparts the Clans hurled themselves in vain all that day and the next.

There were no trees in this part of Malme River Country from which the Ximchaks might have constructed ladders, rams or other siege equipment. So they tried to take the walls by storm and also to taunt or tempt the long-armed Brigands out into the open. The Voygych were stupid savages, but not that stupid. They stayed safe and secure atop the walls of their borrowed city, occasionally dropping paving stones from the top of the walls to crack the skulls of those Ximchaks who didn't dodge fast enough, and nailing others with those darts they used so skillfully, whenever a climbing Ximchak got close enough to the upper works to be a potential danger.

After two days of this, Ganelon's scouts observed a force of Voygych coming downriver from the next city, Lemmery, to find out what all the commotion was about.

His Kuzaks tied ornith reins and nguamadon bridles together into a triple-strand barrier of tough leather, stretching it across the Phrene and effectively blocking passage downriver. The barges of the Lemmery Brigands clustered in midstream, caught in his hastily improvised net, and his Hoy and Fartha archers cut the confused Voygych to pieces.

Following this incident, Silvermane ordered two Clans—the Rooxa and the Gurzi—detached from the main body of the Horde, and sent them riding north to lay siege to Lemmery. He wished to avoid being caught in a pincers movement. Otherwise, the River Brigands might have attacked him from front and rear simultaneously.

At least one valuable item of information had been learned from the siege, and that was that Ruzara still lived. King Yottle had her displayed from atop the walls, her long hair blowing in the wind like a silken banner. Probably, the Voygych monarch planned to use her as a hostage: his intention was not yet clear.

On the third day of the siege (well, during the night of the second day, actually), there were two more attempts by the Lemmery Brigands to make a sneak attack against Ganelon's rear. Barges sneaked out of Lemmery under cover of darkness, eluding the Rooxa and Gurzi patrols, and got downriver, only to find that in the interval Ganelon had strengthened his leather-thong river barrier with a broad net made of woven meadow grasses. Grrff, who could see in the dark with his cat's eyes as well as any Voygych Brigand, commanded a party of Kuzak longbowmen. Both Lemmery assaults were beaten off, slain to the last squalling noseless Voygych.

During the third day, while Ganelon conferred with his Warchiefs (which now included his old friend, Wolf Turgo, who had been elevated by popular acclaim to the War- chieftaincy left vacant when Lord Barzik had been killed at the lower Phrene), two members of the Horde were discov- ered to be absent without permission. These were Harsha of the Horn and Ishgadara the Gynosphinx. Sometime during the night, which had been overcast, murky, and moonless, they had left the encampment, probably together.

Remembering Harsha's unrequited passion for Ruzara, Ganelon presumed he understood the reason.

Ishgadara had probably flown the dashing, mischievous young Herald into the city by cover of darkness, since the walls were unscalable.

That afternoon he redoubled the assault, trying to take the main gate. It was made of old, well-seasoned wood, and his new troop of fire-archers could probably ignite the stuff like tinder.

The use of fire-archers was a trick he had learned from ob- serving the defense of the Triple City. The Tripolitarians had employed hollow, easily broken arrowheads of baked clay, filled with liquid phosphorous which burst into flame when the fluid came into contact with air. Ganelon, however, had improved upon the techniques used in Janeel, Hylage and Corascio, by making arrowheads out of *ignium* mined in the mountains wherethrough they had passed on their way to Elfry.

Some titanic convulsion of nature had thrust these moun- tains to the surface of Old Earth, because the strange inflam- matory metal is found only at the planet's core, where, over geological epochs, pure flame is condensed into metal under terrific pressure.*

The only known substance which can insulate against the

* The neoelement *Ignium* is Number 125 on the Periodic Table, with an atomic weight of 278.

heat of exposed *ignium*, Ganelon's old tutor, the Illusionist of Nerelon, had given him to understand, and keep its intense and fiery heat safely dormant, is (for some strange reason) glass.

Coated with thin, easily frangible glass, *ignium*-tipped arrows may without danger be stored or carried. But once loosed against a solid target the glass pulverizes, and the searing heat of the arrowheads, once exposed to the air, can burn through anything, even stone, metal, or porcelain.

Even if the Horde had possessed these *ignium* arrows at the fruitless siege of the Triple City, it would have done them no good. The remarkable Glass Walls surrounding Hylage, Janeel, and Corascio would of course have been resistant to such.

But they worked well at Kajja.

In no time at all the city gate was ablaze. In minutes it was reduced to charcoal. The Urziks went in first, followed by the Kazoolies. And the slaughtering began.

They did not find Ruzara.

Neither did they discover Ishgadara or Harsha of the Horn.

King Yottle was absent, too.

And *that* was interesting. . . .

It had not been very difficult for the Herald to persuade Ishgadara to lend her wings to his daring escapade.

The Gynosphinx was fond of the Gompish girl, and was bored by inaction. Mounted on her broad warm back, Harsha flew over the walls of Kajja without being sighted by the Voygych.

"Where we goingk?" inquired Ishy in her husky, rasping voice, once they were circling the city streets. That was an unanswerable question: Harsha had no way of knowing in which of the many buildings of Kajja the Brigand had imprisoned Ruzara.

"Fly around for a while and let me puzzle it out," he suggested. She shrugged amiably, observing that she had "alla time in da world."

Under ordinary circumstances, Harsha would have deemed it likely that, as the Brigands' only (and therefore most important) captive, King Yottle had Ruzara under lock and key and personal scrutiny. Also, the large central edifice of the city would probably have been commandeered by the Voygych monarch for his own uses.

But these were *not* ordinary circumstances, and the River Brigands were not civilized people, but ignorant and superstitious savages. Therefore, their behavior patterns could not be predicted with any noteworthy degree of accuracy, even by a Ximchak Barbarian.

Hence it seemed likely to Harsha that the Brigands, who were hardly numerous enough to occupy the entirety of the Empty City, huddled together in one particular quarter of the abandoned Malmanian metropolis. He counted the cooking fires, and directed Ishgadara's flight toward what seemed to him the most populous area.

In the murky darkness it was not difficult for the Gynosphinx to land on a rooftop in this area unseen and unheard. From the parapet they peered down. The streets were choked with debris, and filthy with reeking garbage. The cooking fires were in the streets, with the slovenly Voygych Brigands squatting around them, wolfing down their provender.

As Ruzara was nowhere in view, Harsha began scouting about for her. Warning Ishgadara to stay where she was and to keep out of sight, the young Herald clambered down the ornate stonework at the rear of the building, entered an unshuttered window, and searched the edifice from top to bottom without, however, discovering any trace of the captive girl.

Instead, he got captured himself.

The floor gave way beneath him, dropping Harsha into an empty cellar. He landed unhurt, though with a noisy clatter, and found himself quite effectively trapped. The wooden stairs leading up to the cellar door had evidently rotted away years ago, and there was no means by which he could climb out of the cellar into which his unexpected fall had precipitated him.

He was engaged in trying to rig a ladder of sorts out of the rotten, termite-gutted floor timbers which had fallen in with him, when a ring of grinning, noseless faces appeared at the hole in the floor above. Obviously, the clatter occasioned by the collapsing floor had roused the nearer of the Brigands, who entered the building to investigate.

And now they had *two* Ximchak captives.

Ruzara was first surprised, then scornful, when they threw Harsha in with her.

"What are *you* doing here?" she demanded in astonishment.

"Rescuing you, Princess," he said, grinning. Nothing could for very long daunt Harsha's cheerful spirits, not even capture by the enemy.

"You came into Kajja to rescue me?" she repeated, surprised to discover daring and gallantry in one she had long considered ineffectual and unheroic. He nodded.

"I assure you," the Herald chuckled, "that I would have crept into this vile den of Voygych for no lesser reason. Flew in, actually: Ishgadara helped."

"Ishy? She's here? Have they taken her, too?"

"Not that I know of," he replied. "I think she's still hidden on a rooftop."

Looking him over, she saw no bruises, blood or battlewear. Her red lips formed a scornful *moue*.

"I see you made no protest against your capture," she said scathingly. He shrugged.

"None was possible," he admitted.

"You are certainly no Silvermane!"

"No, I am not," he said agreeably. "On the other hand, Ganelon is no Harsha."

Ruzara avoided making the obvious rejoinder, her spirits too low to get much enjoyment out of mocking him. Besides, he was presently paying no attention to her, busied with examining the door of their cell. It was a massive affair of solid wood.

"If you're thinking of breaking it down or something, you can save your effort," she remarked wearily. "I've already tried everything I could think of. And the hinges are on the outside."

"No, actually I was thinking of burning our way out," he said serenely.

And, removing a flat, cloth-wrapped package from under

his jerkin, he unfolded it and showed her two glass-sheathed *ignium* arrowheads.

She stared at them, then lifted her eyes to look into his friendly, cheerful features, seeing him in a new way.

He had been right in what he had said a moment before. If he was no brawny superman like Ganelon Silvermane, it was equally so that Silvermane, for all his strength and courage, was no keen, quick-witted, clever Harsha. For to bring the *ignium* arrowheads with him would never have occurred to the Warlord.

They were halfway out of the city in the direction of Lemmery before King Yottle caught them.

Since the Ximchak Hordesmen were by now battering away at the gates of Kajja, the day being well advanced by this time, King Yottle decided to simply keep on going.

Overland routes were uncomfortable for the Voygych. Their short bow legs made ornith-riding difficult if not hazardous—their legs weren't long enough to reach the stirrups, and they tended to fall out of the saddle with depressing frequency—and boating down the many rivers of Malme Country was so much easier. Still, the river was patrolled, and just this once Yottle decided to do it the hard way.

They walked, Yottle's royal guard prodding the exhausted boy and girl on ahead. Long before they came within sight of Lemmery they knew the Ximchaks had been here long before them, and from the noise and smoke it was obvious that this city, too, was under siege.

So Yottle took a side route, found the nearest river, which was the Renoza, and, finding Voygych barges docked in the shallows, entered them with his prisoners and men.

They would have to pole against the current all the way, but the Renoza would take them north to Serrium or possibly Uroph.

As far as fat, apprehensive Yottle was concerned, either was all right, but Uroph was farther away, and the farther away from the invading army it was, the better he liked it.

The value of his hostages had largely evaporated by now, but he let the two young persons live, having a new use for them.

So Ruzara and Harsha poled the barges all the way.

It took Ganelon's Ximchaks two days to root all of the River Brigands out of Kajja, and to search the Empty City until he was satisfied his missing comrades were nowhere concealed therein.

Then he led the Horde north to Lemmery, where the two Clans had held the city in siege without yet being able to get through the walls. A second deployment of his fire-archers took them through the wooden gates of Lemmery as easily as they had burned their way into Kajja, and again there was fighting in the streets and on the rooftops, and a fearful slaughter before the last lingering Brigands were pried out of their various hidey-holes.

When cornered, the usually yellow-livered Voygych made vicious fighters, and the toll their darts took of the invaders was heavy. The army had lost eight hundred men in the taking of Kajja and Lemmery, and there were still two Voygych cities to go.

After three days spent in the seizing and sacking of Lemmery, the Horde went north again, arriving before Serrium on the twentieth day since they had entered the Malme River Country. This time the Ximchaks managed to tempt the Voygych out of their walls and into a good, old-fashioned battle. Actually, it was the River Brigands' own idea. Fugitives, fleeing the destruction of the two southern cities, had apprised their brethren in Serrium of the remarkable ease wherewith the invaders had burned their way into the fallen cities through their wooden gates.

And Serrium had wooden gates.

So, when the vanguard of the Horde approached within sight of Serrium, they were attacked from all sides by furious, squalling bands of little bowlegged no-noses. The Voygych employed their dart weapons with the usual devastating effect, but after the initial surprise of the ambush, the Ximchak archers wiped the dartsmen out, and the cavalry slaughtered the rest.

Arrows fly a lot farther than darts may be hurled, as the ignorant Brigands discovered to their sorrow.

When once the nerve of the Voygych broke, it broke for good. Shattered in the brief, bloody battle, the Brigands dispersed in every direction, fleeing in complete disorder, and in their panic few of them had the presence of mind to get back within the relative safety of the walls of Serrium.

This enabled Ganelon Silvermane to take possession of Serrium without difficulty or delay or further losses, and to search it quickly and efficiently. This took the remainder of the day and most of the evening.

That night they camped within Serrium, most of them, anyway.

The following morning they started out for Uroph, last of the Empty Cities known to be in the hands of the Voygych.

And on the way they encountered Ishgadara!

The sphinx-girl was tired and dirty and disheveled, her mane in a sorry condition, her wing-feathers badly in need of a grooming. They gave her food and drink and questioned her, while she gobbled.

When Harsha still had not come back by early afternoon, and the Ximchaks were battling through the streets, Ishgadara had followed a hunch and gone searching by air.

Some hours of flying in ever-widening circles brought her within eyeshot of the two barges toiling up the Renoza. Night was almost upon the world by then, and in the murk she lost sight of them, but returned with word they were heading for Uroph.

This was chilling news.

Uroph was where the Great God Glugluck lived, as the city was built on the shores of Lake Parge. And if King Yottle was fleeing into Uroph, it boded ill for his captives.

For it was to the giant fish that the Voygych were accustomed to sacrifice their captives, when they had captives.

And they had a couple now.

18.

THE GREAT GOD GLUGLUCK

Neither Ruzara nor Harsha got a chance to see very much of Uroph when they finally reached it after weary, exhausting days of poling the heavy-laden barges north against the current.

In the first place it was too late at night by the time they got there to observe much, and they were both so tired they could hardly keep their eyes open.

Yottle had them flung into prison first off, then waddled away on his fat little legs to confer with his brother monarch, King Foosh.* The weary couple fell asleep almost immediately, and did not awaken for many hours.

Yottle had cleverly divided his two captives between the two barges he had commandeered. Had he done otherwise, keeping them both together on the same barge, it was likely that Harsha and Ruzara would have thrown themselves overboard into the river. They couldn't swim, of course, but

---

* There had also been a third Voygych kinglet, according to the Eleventh Commentary on the Epic, a certain King Merve. He is not, however, mentioned in the text of the Epic proper, and I have no idea whatever became of him. He ruled the River Brigands of Lemmery and Serrium, apparently.

they would probably have been willing to take their chances on drowning, just for the opportunity to get away from their Voygych captors.

When they awoke at last, still tired but rested and much refreshed, there was food and drink beside the door. It wasn't much to speak of—black bread and grazer-milk—but they were hungry enough to have tried eating a grazer raw.

The bread was stale and the pale-green grazer-milk had curdled and gone sour, which suggested to one as quick-witted as Harsha that they might have slept the clock around. (Of course, the Gondwanians didn't have clocks in this age, but you know what I mean.)

Since there was nothing else to do after polishing off this feeble excuse for a breakfast down to the last black crumb and green droplet, they sat back to wait for something to happen.

Harsha had carried off only two of the *ignium* arrowheads from the Ximchak encampment, so they couldn't escape by the same trick they had used earlier.

One arrowhead had been used in burning through the cell door, and Harsha had spent the second in starting a diversionary fire to lure the Voygych in the wrong direction. The trick had not worked for long, but he still thought it had been a good idea.

They dozed after a time.

There was nothing else for them to do but wait.

Ganelon feared that the superstitious River Brigands might well decide to sacrifice their captives to their Glassfish god, since to their way of thinking the Ximchak invasion was probably a token of his wrath, which they could perhaps propitiate with a dual sacrifice. But there was little or nothing that he could do to prevent this from happening.

It would take his fastest ornithmen five days to get from Serrium to Uroph, and by the time they got there Ruzara and the Herald would probably be digesting in Glugluck's stomach, or, anyway, have long since drowned.

The trouble was one of terrain. It was not by idle whim that the Malmanians, and after them the Voygych, adopted modes of transport almost completely riparian in nature. While the distance between the two Empty Cities was not great, innumerable streams and lakes and rivers made the going (by foot) slow and difficult.

Yet there were no barges left to accommodate the host, all having been either burned by the Ximchaks or taken into Uroph. And there were no stands of trees in the vicinity from which to construct rafts. And, anyway, river travel was an exceedingly complicated business of maneuvering upstream here, downstream there, and seesawing back and forth to get anywhere.

So, while the main body of the Horde tramped along on foot or in the saddle, gingerly fording the streams and using makeshift rope bridges to traverse the broader rivers, he and Grrff and Kurdi set off for Uroph aboard their winged friend, Ishgadara.

There was little the four of them could do to prevent or postpone the sacrifice of Harsha and the Gompish girl. But what little they could do, they grimly intended to do.

As for the Voygych, they were in an uproar. Such a calamity as this invasion by a vast army had never before interrupted the placid, age-old way of life they had heretofore enjoyed. They were accustomed to preying on others, and quite unprepared to have the tables turned like this.

It seemed to King Foosh that his Brigands had already tried everything they could think of to discourage or drive away the invaders. They had holed up behind their borrowed city walls, only to have the Ximchaks besiege them, which eventually resulted in slaughter.

They had tried striking at the Ximchak Barbarians by river in their attack-barges, choosing the darkest nights possible, but this hadn't worked too well either, and eventually resulted in more slaughter of Voygych.

They had even gone to the extremity of trying to fight off the Ximchaks in land battles. This had ended up in the same gory manner as the other ways they had tried. To their limited intellects, there was nothing left to try.

It was Yottle who suggested they feed their two Ximchak prisoners to the lake god. Glugluck was by way of being his own personal discovery, for, many years ago, when first the Voygych had entered Malme River Country a footweary gaggle of homeless vagabonds, it had been he, Yottle, who first identified the huge Glassfish in Lake Parge with the im-memorial divinity worshipped by the Voygych.

The other Voygych had accepted his notion without dis-pute, and the great Glassfish didn't seem to object to having divine honors paid to him, so everybody was happy.

But now was the time to coax a miracle out of the Incar-nate Glugluck, if ever they needed one.

The first intimation Ruzara or Harsha had of the impend-ing religious ceremony in which, so to speak, they would be the main course was when a troop of ungainly Voygych maidens came to prepare them.

A ritual bath was the first step, and Harsha, being a Ximchak all the way, protested vigorously. So vigorously that the Voygych vestals had to summon a few bullyboys to hold him down while they stripped, immersed, and scrubbed him, giggling all the while. (The vestals did the giggling: Harsha made vocal his resentment by yelling lustily. The Ximchaks were not accustomed to bathing, believing that their manly vigor depended on the retention of their epidermal oils.)

Ruzara suffered the indignity of comparable lustrations in tight-lipped silence. To tell the truth, it had been longer than she could remember since she had enjoyed a good hot bath. And, had it not been for her suspicion that this welcome cleansing was but the prelude to a grimmer rite, she would have wallowed in the soapy water, luxuriating.

Once washed and dried, and even perfumed, the two were robed in skimpy white kaftans which bore a distinct resem-blance to shrouds. Then they were paraded through the gar-bage-choked streets of Uroph, being pelted with flowers all the way, down to the lakefront.

Glugluck had been aroused from his diurnal nap by means of castanets and clickers, a staccato music of sorts which the Voygych punctuated erratically by thumping on drums and gongs. The huge lake-dweller was cruising around the end of the pier, goggling curiously at the festive crowds. He knew something was up, but feared it was just another indigestible meal of uncooked human. On the whole, he preferred a blander diet of nice algae, spiced, occasionally, with tadpoles.

Harsha and Ruzara were prodded out onto the pier at the end of long poles, and thus got their first look at the fish god of the Brigands. They goggled at him with much the same round-eyed curiosity with which he was observing the goings-on.

In the first place, Glugluck was probably the biggest Glassfish either of them had ever seen, or anybody else in Gondwane, for that matter; and in the second place, he was a Glassfish.

Glassfish are so named because they are almost entirely transparent, far more lucent than any jellyfish. So transparent, in fact, that their internal organs are clearly visible, looking rather like a hodge-podge of cellophane bags bundled inside of a huge hollow glass tank.

That big bulb toward the rear was Glugluck's stomach. The greenish muck sloshing around within it was the residue of Glugluck's breakfast. The glassy knot up toward the front that kept going *boomp-boomp-boomp* was his heart.

Everything about Glugluck, on his outside or his inside, was equally transparent, his brain (which was of considerable size, as he was a most sagacious old fish) resembling lucent pink jelly, while his curved ribs looked like transparent tubes. He was quite a thing to see, was Glugluck.

The matter of his size was equally interesting. For six hundred and sixty-seven years Glugluck had lived at the bottom of Lake Parge (not counting an occasional trip up- or downriver when he got bored seeing the same old scenery all the time), and for all of that span he had continued to grow and grow until by now he was about as big as a modest-size ship.

So big, in fact, that he looked fully capable of swallowing them whole, if he took it in his mind to do so. Ruzara shuddered at the thought, and pressed close to Harsha. Harsha wished mightily that he could put his arms around her, but as his wrists were tied behind his back there was little chance of this.

The Voygych, hoarsely voicing praise of Glugluck, continued to prod the two reluctant sacrifices with their long poles, until the two had reached the very end of the stone pier. One more good prod would push them in, and they would sink swiftly to the bottom unless swallowed by Glugluck. Lead weights tied to the bottoms of their sacrificial robes would ensure that this happened.

Glugluck was a wise old fish, philosophical in his fishy way, and knew what all this was about. He had observed similar ceremonies at frequent intervals throughout the Voygych tenure, although such had never happened while the Malmanians had been in residence. They had made a huge pet of him, for being a strict vegetarian, he was of placid and unsavage temperament, as friendly as a dolphin or porpoise.

He recalled with nostalgic affection how the Malmanian youths and maidens had swum and sported about him during their Water Festivals, and how the more daring of the young people had even ridden astride his back on occasion. Those had been happy times for Glugluck, although of course he had been called by a different name in those days.

More than once a chubby Malmanian child had by accident fallen into Lake Parge, and Glugluck fondly remembered how pleased the grown-ups had been when, on such events, he had plucked the fat little persons out of the water and had held them high and reasonably dry in his mouth until the older swimmers could reach them. At such times the Malmanians had rewarded him with fresh honeyblossoms, uncooked succulents, a variety of juicy tubers, and other vegetarian rarities which afforded him an interestingly varied diet for many days.

Hence, when the Voygych pushed the helpless duo into the lake, Glugluck snatched them up in friendly fashion.

Harsha and the girl had breathed their last prayer to the gods just before hitting the water: now, finding themselves scooped up in the mouth of the monster Glassfish, they did not at first know whether they were saved or were about to join the rest of Glugluck's breakfast.

The mouth of Glugluck was fat and soft, with pillowy thick lips of transparent blubber, and, as the two quickly discerned, his jaws had no teeth in them. In fact, peering down Glugluck's throat, they saw that however wide his mouth and jaws, his gullet soon narrowed into a tube which led to an orifice far too small for him to swallow any part of them, except perhaps a hand or a foot. And, as Glugluck was holding his head up out of the water—at least for the moment—they were in no danger of being drowned.

"Great Galendil," breathed Harsha incredulously, "I think the huge fellow is trying to save our lives!"

Ruzara's teeth were chattering, but she managed to say something to the effect that if she ever got out of this predicament in one piece, she swore never to eat fish again as long as she lived.

The Voygych were at first overwhelmed with joy that their divine Glassfish had accepted the sacrifices, then plunged into dismay to see that he was actually rescuing them. They were accustomed to the minor disappointment of watching him let sacrifices drown, for usually Glugluck ignored the people who were tossed in to him. But today, for some reason, Glugluck was in a playful, good-humored mood, remembering how the nice Malmanians had rewarded him on similar occasions with a tasty salad.

Alarmed, the Voygych piled into their balsa barges and coasted out onto the lake, waving their long anthropoid arms and yelling and ringing loud bells. Obviously, they hoped to agitate Glugluck to such a point that the big fish would swallow his mouthful of sacrifices down.

Glugluck, however, became annoyed. Still carefully holding his mouth up out of the water, the enormous marine creature sailed about in a lazy circle, overturning the small wedge-shaped barges with easy, playful flips of his tailfins. Yelping Brigands fell in the water, floundering and squalling in an ecstasy of fear.

It is one thing to encourage one's fishy divinity into swallowing people alive. It becomes a slightly different matter when one of those people may, possibly, include oneself.

It was this extraordinary spectacle which confronted Grrff, Kurdi and Ganelon when they arrived at length over Uroph, mounted on the sphinx-girl's back.

The waters of Lake Parge were littered with overturned barges, drifting aimlessly to and fro, and dotted with the bald, red-painted heads of soggy, unhappy Voygych. In the midst of all this confusion, Glugluck swam idly in small, lazy circles, carefully holding Harsha and Ruzara up out of the water.

Ganelon Silvermane quite naturally assumed that his helpless friends were in the clutches, well, the jaws, then, of a carnivorous monster, and was about to put an *ignium*-tipped arrow into the Great God Glugluck, which would doubtless have broiled the poor creature on the spot.

Ishgadara, however, bade him stay his hand. The Gynosphinx, herself more beast than human, recognized the sentience which gleamed in the affable, goggling orbs of Glugluck. She pointed out how deliberately he was holding his head up in order not to let the water enter his half-open mouth.

Ganelon felt helpless. "What do we do, then? How do we get them out of the jaws of that monster?"

Ishy dipped lower, zooming over the head of the Glassfish.

"Hey, pig* fish, you spittingk um out, now!" she roared in her stentorian foghorn voice.

Glugluck was becoming short-tempered and testy by this time. It was bad enough having one's lifesaving attempts rewarded by yellings and bangings, without being dive-bombed by Gynosphinxes. So the Glassfish made for the nearer shore, poked his huge head up onto the beach, and disgorged the two humans as gently as he could manage.

Then, with a last flirt of his enormous tail, which tossed a half-dozen luckless Voygych into the air, the friendly fish dove to the bottom of the lake, firmly resolved to partake in no further Voygych festivities for a fortnight, at least.

Ishgadara landed, and Ganelon and Grrff hopped down to see how their friends were, after this harrowing ordeal. The two were somewhat waterlogged, and smelled heavily of Fish, and were shaken, but otherwise unharmed. Grrff cut their bonds with a *snick* of his sharp, strong claws, while Kurdi and the sphinx-girl kept a weather eye peeled for River Brigands. But these unhappy persons were too busy trying to fish their half-drowned compatriots out of the drink to bother trying to recapture their prisoners.

The Gynosphinx could not carry five, but luckily Glugluck had disgorged Harsha and Ruzara on the far side of the lake, away from Uroph, so an overland escape was feasible. Letting the Gompish girl and the Herald fly astride Ishgadara with little Kurdi, who didn't weigh enough to matter, they lit

---

* Ishgadara implied no insult to Glugluck by this usage. She was congenitally unable to pronounce the letter *B*.

out in the direction of Serrium, with Ganelon and Grrff running along underneath.

Whenever they came to a river or stream too deep to be easily forded afoot, Ganelon would swim over with Grrff clinging unhappily to his back. The Tigerman had inherited from his feline ancestry an intense dislike of water. Once they had put a fairish distance between themselves and Uroph, and it became apparent the Voygych were not pursuing them, they simply sat down and waited for the advance guard of the Horde to arrive.

That took three days or so.

Continuing on to Uroph again, at the head of his Ximchaks, Ganelon arrived before the city to discover that all of the fight was gone from the Voygych. Yottle had been among those drowned in Lake Parge when Glugluck overturned the barges, and this disastrous event, together with Glugluck's very deliberate and meaningful rejection of the sacrifices, had been interpreted as omens distinctly unfavorable to the Voygych opposition to the Ximchak invasion.

Over the next day or two surrender terms were agreed upon, and Ganelon permitted the remnants of the Voygych River Brigands to leave the country unharmed. As reparations for the losses suffered by the Ximchaks, the Voygych listlessly turned over all of the loot and plunder amassed by their brigandage to be divided between the Nine Clans.

To make sure they never returned to bother future travelers in Malme River Country again, Silvermane ordered their balsa barges burned to ashes.

Then the Horde turned around and marched out of this region, choosing a route less interrupted by rivers, and rather regretting their hasty incineration of the river boats.

Ten days later they crossed the border into the lands of the Merdingian Regnate.

19.

THE LAND OF WARRING CITIES

Selestor's map showed Merdingia as a hilly country divided
between the five cities of Spoyda, Urd, Nygosh, Kashpode
and Eryph. The geographies Ganelon had studied back at
Nerelon had reported that the cities of this Regnate were
ruled by hereditary peers. There had once been a dynasty of
kings who had ruled Merdingia for many generations, but
when Murgoyd the Last perished in the Pink Plague, he left
no heir and thus the royal title lapsed.

As they entered the Regnate, it quickly became evident to
them that the various peers had not yet been able to agree on
a successor to the vacant throne. In the absence of a royal
overlord, it seemed the land was at war.

If you could *call* it war, that is.

The Ximchaks burst out laughing as they mounted the
Yadder* Hills, and got their first view of the Siege of
Spoyda.

Exactly thirty-two fat, elderly, gray-headed knights lay en-

* Yadder is a color in the octave of visible light, peculiar to the
Gondwanish spectrum. Several new colors had been added to the chro-
matic spectrum by the Eon of the Falling Moon.

camped before the gates of Spoyda, the mauve-and-silvern pennants of Duke Wuliam of Eryph fluttering bravely atop the tentpoles. From the number of filled-in latrine trenches wherewith the plain was scored, the siege had been in more or less continuous operation for some years.

Traffic, however, continued to trickle in and out of the Spoydan gates, undeterred by the two knights who sat on campchairs to either side, guarding two faded and rather dilapidated signs. One of these read:

SHAME ON SPOYDA FOR NOT RECOGNIZING THE ERYPHIAN CLAIM!

The second was blazoned with this message:

DUKE WULIAM OF ERYPH FOR KING OF ALL THE MERDINGIANS!

Considerable alarums and excursions were noted among the besieging army as the Ximchak host appeared on the hill line. The old knights, most of whom had been enjoying an afternoon snooze in their hammocks, fell out with thumps, and waddled away to fetch their armor, as an attack seemed imminent.

Kuzaks came galloping down the Ximchak line from the Clans situated at either extremity of the Horde's front, reporting that scouts had observed similar activities afoot before two nearby cities.

Kashpode, to the north, was under siege by twenty-eight of the chivalry of Count Motosca of Urd. Placards before that city protested the recalcitrance of the Kashpodeans in refusing to recognize the Count of Urd's claim to the crown.

And a mere sixteen knights, in the puce-and-yellow of Spoyda, held Nygosh to the south under similar siege. Banners posted before Nygosh protested that the true and legal claim of Ferrule, Marquis of Spoyda, was being ignored by the Nygoshians to their dread peril.

Ganelon thought it prudent not to mix in these purely local politics until he knew what was going on. So he ordered the Ximchaks to make camp atop the hills.

That night heralds arrived, much out of breath, having rid-

den from Spoyda with the Marquis Ferrule's offer to pur-
chase the Ximchak services in his war against Nygosh.

During the rest of that evening, and at intervals over the
next two days, similar offers to hire the Ximchaks as mercenaries were received from Count Motosca of Urd, Baron
Zimmerian of Kashpode, Quailos, Earl of Nygosh, and Duke
Wuliam of Eryph.

Ganelon received each of these embassies separately, and
gravely listened to what they had to say. Engaging the heralds in converse, he at length elicited enough basic information so as to form a good idea of exactly what conditions
were here in Merdingia.

It would seem that the people of the Merdingian Regnate
had never exactly been what you might call a warlike race,
and when at last they failed to agree on which of the peer-
ages should most properly succeed the extinct dynasty which
the death of King Murgoyd had left with no heir to inherit,
they found themselves in a quandry.

Honor demanded that each peer press his claim by force, if
necessary. But, while the Merdingians knew the *theory* of
war, they had no experience in the practice of it.

They knew enough about armed contention, however, to
realize that mounting a siege was the very least they could do
to uphold the honor of the peers.

The sieges (there were five of them currently operating)
had been going on now for eighty-seven years.

And if ever there was a realm in need of mercenaries, it
was Merdingia.

It was then that Ganelon got his Idea. . . .

His solution, which served to solve many problems, did not
come to him all at once, but in bits and pieces.

There were many things Ganelon had to worry about.

In the first place, his primary concern in accepting the
leadership of the Horde was to somehow get it out of Greater
Arzenia and start it moving in another direction: otherwise,
his own homeland, Zermish in the Hegemony, was endangered by its very proximity. So, too, were the homelands of
many peoples he considered his friends—Valardus and Tran-

core, Karjixia and the Hegemony as a whole, and the realms and countries around.

This he had managed to do.

His second concern, oddly enough—oddly, that is to say, in light of his first concern above—was the safety and existence of the Horde itself. (Ganelon had taken his vows seriously, and took his responsibilities as Warlord equally seriously.)

Now, the Horde by this time was dangerously depleted. At the point in time when the Ximchaks had occupied Gompery, they had been nearly two hundred thousand strong. Since then, however, heavy losses had cut into their numbers. In part, these losses were his own fault, for he had been associated with the defeats at Valardus, Mount Naroob, the Bryza, and the Ovarva Plains Battle, which had accounted for the demise of fourteen thousand and three hundred Ximchaks.

The last winter spent in Gompery had cost another two hundred lives, and various other hazards such as the Sleeping Forest, the Triple City siege, and the bloody passage through the Narrow Vale between the Warbird Cliffs had taken the lives of a thousand Ximchaks more. Indeed, totaling the number of Ximchak dead came to an appalling number—why, three thousand, seven hundred and seventy-five had died fighting the Strange Little Men of the Hills alone—and another twelve hundred and five had fallen in war, battle, siege, sack, and ambush in Malme River Country.

And this total did not even take into account the normal attrition suffered by the Horde: the dozens who died monthly in duels and drunken quarrels, the scores who had drifted away over the eight months and twelve days the Horde had been on the western march, deserting to become vagabonds or bandits. Nor did Ganelon's count include the Ximchak women who died in childbirth, or who knifed each other over men, the urchins of the Horde who succumbed to injury or illness, the old warriors who died for the reasons old men die in every land and age, nor the dozens and dozens who had perished, over the many months of the Great Migration, from snakebite, avalanche, drowning, fever, untreated wounds, or injuries, or had wandered away and gotten lost, or fallen while crossing the mountains.

By this time, adding it all up, tens of thousands had perished or left the Horde, and its size had been whittled down over the past year to merely that of a good-sized army (by Gondwanish standards, that is).

The once-mighty Ximchak Horde, which had been a peril to the civilized world, was no longer particularly dangerous.

They stayed in these parts of the Merdingian Regnate another thirty days. To exercise his troops, and to let them blow off a little excess steam, during that period Ganelon permitted eight or ten of the various tribes to hire themselves out to the five peers. He saw to it that each mercenary force was evenly matched so that none would enjoy an unfair advantage over the others. They happily skirmished on the grassy plains, surrendering amiably to their fellow-Hordesmen whenever one group in particular had gained a clear tactical advantage.

Few lives were lost and the Merdingian peers were pleased, and everybody had a good time.

Without ever realizing it, Ganelon Silvermane had by pure chance reinvented the kind of gentlemanly warfare-as-an-art-form practiced during the Renaissance by the Italian *condottiere*.

Other tribes he dispatched north, to scout the country up there. They returned about two weeks later, reporting their discovery of interminable grasslands where roamed immense, fat herds of a species of game resembling reindeer—if reindeer had three eyes, no horns, and vestigial wings, that is.

This north country was made for nomad hunters, from the descriptions the scouting parties brought back. It reminded the older veterans of the Horde of their own original country, which some of them had actually seen in their early boyhood, and which others had been told about by their fathers and grandfathers.

This reminded Ganelon Silvermane of a fact he had forgotten: that the now-warlike Ximchaks had originally been peaceful bands of happy nomad hunters, roaming the grassy steppes between the great rivers, Xim and Chak, somewhere in the remote northern parts of Gondwane the Great.

And so, as the bits and pieces fell together, Ganelon conceived of his Idea.

In the meanwhile, as Ganelon slowly worked out his solution to the problem of how to dispose of the Ximchak army in as humane a manner as possible, and without harming the Ximchaks themselves in any way, there occurred a wedding.

Harsha of the Horn and Ruzara of Gompery desired to be wed.

During their captivity together, the impulsive ex-Princess had fallen passionately in love with her daring and gallant (and really quite handsome) young rescuer. His tender and solicitous and very chivalric behavior toward her during their imprisonment together had, in its own way, impressed her as deeply as had his courage and devotion in pursuing her alone into the very stronghold of their enemies.

Harsha and Ruzara were both of the now almost depopulated Gurko Clan, and its new Warchief, Wolf Turgo, was happy to give his permission for the nuptials.

As the Gurkoes were currently in the employment of Lord Ferrule, the Marquis of Spoyda, the Spoydans were persuaded to pick up the tab for the festivities. Indeed, the ceremonies were sumptuous, the feasting lavish, and so many pretty, dark-eyed Spoydan dancing girls entertained at the nuptial celebration and caught the eye of this or that young buck of the Horde, that Ganelon thought it likely more than a few weddings would shortly ensue.

After an evening of dance and feast and music, and a brief, simple exchange of vows before the grave eyes of the Warlord, a proud and beaming Harsha led his demure Gompish bride to a new white tent erected just for their honeymoon.

It was, as Ganelon had guessed it would be, the first of many weddings between young Ximchak bloods and ravishing Spoydan, or Kashpodean, or Nygoshy maidens.

Strangers are always more interesting than the people you grow up with.

They had originally thought only to spend a month in the Merdingian Regnate, resting after their battles in Malme River Country and licking their wounds. But the days went on, the weeks piled up, and they soon discovered, did the Ximchaks, that they were well into the second month.

It was winter by now, and the west and the south borders

of the Regnate were walled by mighty ranges of mountains, and the passes across these mountains soon became blocked by snow, which gave them a good reason for staying awhile longer.

More than a few tribes drifted up into the north country to try their hand at the old, traditional Ximchak sport of hunting. They found, to their surprise, pleasure, and delight, that they were exceptionally skillful at it. Apparently, it ran in the Ximchak blood.

They found the life of hunting camp and the chase healthy, invigorating, and, somehow, deeply satisfying. At night, about the cooking fires, they tried to remember the old, old songs of their nomad grandsires, and raised their young voices to the sharp wintry stars in songs whose words they scarcely understood, but which made them want to weep.

And all of this, Ganelon observed, putting two and two together.

Eventually, he had four.

Eventually, he had thought out his Idea. But he bided his time, waiting to see if the Ximchaks became restive and quarrelsome, and desirous of moving on.

Curiously enough, they did not.

The second month passed even swifter than the first. The Ximchaks—it never even occurred to them to conquer and sack the five Merdingian cities—found themselves gradually drifting apart from each other.

Some of the younger Barbarians, who had by now acquired something more than just a veneer of sophistication from their contacts with the many civilizations they had observed, fought, or passed through, became fascinated by city life. Among these were the Ximchak craftsmen and artisans: they found the shops and bazaars and gardens of Spoyda and Kashpode and Nygosh peculiarly entrancing. More than a few quit the Horde to live in the three central cities of the Regnate.

They found themselves welcomed, and that heartily. The Merdingians were a friendly and hospitable people, interested in travelers, and thoroughly devoid of the provincial xenophobia common to other, more isolated realms.

Even the young warriors, and more than a few of the middle-aged ones, began to drift away, finding themselves

brides among the Merdingian ladies. Even this caused no resentment among the Merdingian gentlemen, who themselves
found some of the unmarried wenches of the Horde extraordinarily attractive, with their bright scarlet eyes, mischievous
flirting ways, and warm, chocolate skins.

At first a dozen or so weddings were performed in the
Horde. Then dozens more. Finally, it got to be a common
event.

The Horde was melting away.

The more warlike of the Hordesmen, those who did not
find city life interesting, or who found it too confining, enjoyed the maneuverings and skirmishes of the mercenaries
more to their liking. These martial activities had all the dash
and flourish and excitement of war, without any of the pain
and sweat, the anguish and the bloodshed.

And the peaceable Merdingian peers, who were paying the
mercenaries, were just as pleased to score a purely strategic
victory over their rival claimants for the empty throne as to
win an actual battle.

The fact of the matter was, quite simply, that the contention for the Merdingian crown had by now become a game, a
mere pastime, to the five peers, and they would all have been
reluctant to see it end.

Another thirty days drifted by in this manner, with the
Ximchaks marrying Merdingian girls and settling down to
city life, or busying themselves in the elaborate wargames the
mercenary contests had become, or resuming the old
Ximchak ways of life as nomad hunting bands in the north.

Winter was over by now, and the passes into the south and
west were cleared of the snows which had blocked passage
through them, but no one suggested they be moving on.

Eight more days went by, and it became time to celebrate
a certain anniversary. For that eighth day of the Horde's
fourth month in Merdingia marked the precise end of the
Ximchaks' first year on their Great Migration.

And Ganelon called a Great Council of all the Warchiefs,
and tribal chieftains and subchiefs.

And told them he wished to dissolve the Horde.

20.

GANELON SILVERMANE DEPARTS

Ganelon's opening words to the Council, announcing his purpose in convening them, occasioned consternation, alarm, and surprise. He followed his first words with a simple, straightforward description of what had begun to happen within the Horde during its visit to the Merdingian Regnate. It was Ganelon's notion to accept what was already happening, and to implement it.

"Those of our young men, and our more mature warriors as well, who feel attracted to city life should be openly encouraged to become Merdingian citizens," he said gravely. "The five peers, and the city folk in general, have already demonstrated their willingness to accept Ximchaks among them. Marriages have been arranged, the young warriors wooing unmarried Merdingian maidens, the older men courting widows."

"That a Ximchak should ever deign to live within city walls!" sighed Lord Ruzik of Tharrad dolefully.

"But many of them already are," Ganelon said reasonably. "And many more wish to. There is nothing innately wrong with accepting the protection afforded by city walls, or the social code that makes civilized life tolerable. Living within a city does not unman a warrior, or make him effete or cowardly. You know this from your own experience, Lord Ruzik: the city dwellers of Valardus and Kan Zar Kan, of Trancore and the Triple City, proved this beyond all questioning, in the losses they exacted from the Horde."

"Um," said Ruzik of Tharrad.

"And," continued Silvermane, "for those who have found the nomadic hunting life of the northern plains to their taste, there is no reason why they should not be encouraged to adopt those ways permanently."

"That a Ximchak should chase reindeer instead of bravely facing the hosts of the foe!" sighed Lord Arnhelm the Kazooli disparagingly.

"It requires no less bravery to face a herd of stampeding beasts than a resolute human foe," Ganelon pointed out firmly. "And, Lord Arnhelm, it ill befits one whose noble and dauntless ancestors thrived on the hardy life of nomad hunters, before being roused to war, to denigrate that life. It was good enough for your own grandsires, you know."

"Um," said Arnhelm of Kazool.

"On the other hand, for those of our seasoned warriors who truly prefer the field of war to the stimulus of civilization or the excitement of hunting, there remains the honorable, the manly, and the extremely lucrative profession of arms in service to the contending peers of Merdingia as mercenaries. They can enjoy all the glamor, the swagger, the color and regimen of military life in that profession, relieved, for the most part, of the blood and sweat, the crippling wounds, the anguish over the death of comrades, that war usually affords those who follow her."

"That a Ximchak should merely play at war!" sighed Lord Dygoth of the Rooxas sadly.

"There is really nothing intrinsically noble, courageous or glorious about fighting," Ganelon reminded him. "Warfare only becomes noble when fought with chivalry, among gentlemen. It only displays courage when a few make a bold stand against many. And glory only follows upon the heels of victory. These precise elements are found in mercenary warfare as often as in ordinary wars of conquest or aggrandizement, Lord Dygoth."

"Um," said Dygoth of Rooxa.

"I propose, therefore, that these suggestions be put to the Horde fairly and openly and without prejudice, so that every single Ximchak be able to choose which of the three new life modes best suits his ambitions and appetites. And, for those few who may select to continue the Horde life mode they have become accustomed to, they may organize under a chosen leader, and continue on the Great Migration into the west. For the rest of us, however, the Clans should be dissolved into their component tribes, and the tribes adopt the mode of life they prefer in the time to come."

"That the mighty Ximchak Horde should ever disband, break up, come apart!" sighed Lord Drogo of the Qarrs woefully.

"You forget, Lord Drogo, that the Horde has always been an unnatural alliance, artificially constructed out of previously free and independent tribes and Clans," reminded Ganelon. "These were welded together by the political genius of the Warlord Xoden, and trained to fight together by the military genius of the Warlord Zaar. But, for all that, the Horde is no less a synthetic union of different peoples, and always has been. The natural state of the Ximchak peoples is a loose confederacy of free and sovereign tribes."

"Um," said Drogo Oneeye of the Qarrs.

"Once the matter has been proposed to the Horde, and put to a vote, no longer will there be any need or necessity for a Warlord, and I intend to lay down my duties and travel south with my friends Grrff and Ishgadara and Kurdi," continued Ganelon. "Those disputes which arise between the tribes or Clans in the future can best be settled by the leaders in council met: without wars to fight, you no longer require a Warlord. And I have been too long away from home as it is."

"That a Ximchak Warlord should abdicate!" sighed Wolf Turgo of the Gurkoes mournfully.

"I have fulfilled the purposes for which I accepted the duties of your Warlord," Ganelon pointed out gravely. "I led the Horde out of the Gompish Regime safely and honorably, without retreating; I led you into the west where you could discover your own individual destinies, and I have put an end to the mad career of world conquest to which the overweening ambitions of Zaar would have perverted you. I have done everything that I promised I would do; and now I want to go home."

"Um," said Turgo the Gurko.

Many days and nights of discussion, proposal, argument and counterproposal followed, for none of the Warchiefs, mindful of his own importance, could safely accept the Warlord's decision without at least the appearance of serious, thoughtful, and weighty ponderings of this important matter.

But in the end it was decided to implement the suggestion of Ganelon Silvermane, and the matter was put to the Horde for vote, warrior by warrior, family by family, tribe by tribe, and Clan by Clan. And so it came to pass that the Horde agreed to disband, each man choosing the way of life that most appealed to him.

Over the next three months the once-mighty Horde gradually came apart at the seams.

Twenty or thirty thousand of the Ximchaks drifted north, to adopt the hardy, invigorating life of nomad huntsmen their ancestors had followed from time immemorial. The vast and empty North Plains had room enough for all.

Another twenty or thirty thousand entered into the various cities of Merdingia, some choosing to settle in Kashpode, others in Nygosh, more in Urd, a few in Eryph, and quite a large number in Spoyda. Marquis Ferrule, Baron Zimmerian, Earl Quaolis, Count Motosca, and Duke Wuliam hospitably made them feel welcome.

Some became smiths, others tanners, weavers, or dyers. As well, jewelers and pottery-makers, fletchers and wainwrights, minstrels and poets, merchants and tradesmen, artisans and ornith-breeders, came from among those of the Ximchaks who had followed, or who had desired to follow, those professions while members of the Horde.

An even larger contingent of former Ximchaks formed new armies as mercenaries, and permitted themselves to be hired by the peers of the five cities.

And those who stubbornly desired to continue the old, familiar Horde ways of conquest and war reformed into new groupings, and marched away into the west, perhaps to find kingdoms to rule.

As for the Kuzaks, Ganelon commanded that they disband

and never again reform. This was very much against their own wishes, but Ganelon persevered, and so great was their love for him that they reluctantly obeyed this last wish from him who had been their first and only tribal chieftain.

"More than I have prized my title of Warlord of the Ximchak Horde, I have treasured the honor of being chieftain of the Kuzak tribe," Ganelon told them simply, on the occasion of their dissolution. "I am not willing that, ever again, another chieftain should lead my Kuzaks, be it in peace or be it in war. I shall be proud to hold the title of your chieftain until I die."

Eleven days after this, Ganelon took his own departure out of the land of the Merdingian cities. It was two years to the very day since he had first taken the vows and become a Ximchak Hordesman.

He did it secretly, and by night, so that none should mark his going, and so that none could follow him.

For he very much feared that some of his Kuzaks, in disobedience to their promise, would ride after him, to share in his great journey south. In particular, he feared the Champions would not willingly let him go.

Earlier that same evening he had feasted his dearest friends and fellow-warriors, bidding each of them goodbye. Bargon the Kazooli and Thrag of Tharrad were too choked with emotion to do more than wring his hand in their strong grip. Varax the Gurziman and Partha the Fartha had wept openly. Jumba of the Hoys and Khon the Rooxa had gotten very drunk. And Yurkham the Urziki and Nabbad of Qarr had embraced him in a last farewell.

Also present, along with Grrff, was Wolf Turgo. No longer was he Lord Turgo, for the Gurkoes had split into four factions, each choosing one of the alternatives open to the Horde, and since there was no longer a Clan for him to lead, there was no longer any need for a Warchief to lead it.

He and Ganelon shook hands somberly, making their farewells.

"I shall miss you, big fellow," admitted Turgo. "Remember, I knew you first, before any of 'em; back in Trancore, it was, back before the Ovarva Massacre. We've been friends a long time, and it's hard to say goodbye. . . ."

"I know," said Ganelon heavily. Then he asked: "You forgot to tell me what you have decided to do: is it the hunt for you, or the field of war, or what?"

Wolf grinned embarrassedly.

"I went into Spoyda to visit Harsha and his mate last week," he said. "They have a little house with a garden, and there's a child on the way, you know."

Ganelon nodded.

"Well ... they had neighbors from down the street in to meet me. And there was a girl. Prettier than Lady Ruzara, *I* think! Anyway, quieter and easier to get along with. Big black eyes, and hair like silk, and a soft, low voice. It did funny things up and down my backbone, that voice. Zara, her name is; father's in the caravan trade. Could use a fellow to handle his orniths—and I was always pretty good handling orniths."

"Could also use a son-in-law, maybe?" grinned Silvermane.

The other flushed, then grinned back.

"Maybe so. We'll see."

Ganelon clapped him on the back.

"Well, goodbye, and good luck, whatever happens. I shall not soon forget you, friend," said Silvermane.

"Nor I, you," said Wolf Turgo of the Gurko Clan.

That very night Ganelon Silvermane, and Grrff the Xombolian, and the boy Kurdi, with all their gear, climbed astride the broad, furry back of Ishgadara and soared up into the moonless sky, and circled into the south.

It had been a long time since Ganelon had left his home in the enchanted palace of Nerelon among the Crystal Mountains.

He wanted to see again his old master, the Illusionist, and little Phadia, the boy he had rescued from the Puerium of Shai in the Land of Red Magic, and the talkative and motherly Bazonga-bird, that amazing, animated vehicle.

And he wanted to take a brief trip north of Nerelon into the Hegemony, to visit his foster father, Phlesco the Godmaker, and his foster mother, Imminix the Pseudowoman, and see again all the old, familiar sights of Zermish, the city in which he had been raised.

He had reached, at this point in his life, no conclusion as

to the shape or the direction of his future career, and had no idea of the purpose to which he ought to devote himself.

Probably, there would be a lot more adventures.

But first, he wanted to go home.

He thought about the Ximchaks. They had not really been his people, although he had come to like and respect them, and to feel concerned about their well-being. *Funny how an enemy can turn into a friend, once you get to know him,* he thought to himself.

And he thought about the Kuzaks, and the eight Champions. They had not really been his people, either, but they had been his comrades-in-arms, his men, his friends, his brothers.

And he loved them. . . .

They flew on into the unknown south, beneath the starry skies of Gondwane, where strange adventures among new people awaited them, while Grrff, seated in the rear, with Kurdi on his lap, made a great business about pointing out the different stars and constellations to the boy, naming them one by one, and chatting about them loudly.

They pretended to ignore Ganelon, because he was weeping, his great head lowered on his mighty breast, and they did not want to embarrass him by noticing.

The
Appendix

A Glossary of Places
Mentioned in the Text

Note: The following Glossary includes natural features, such as mountains, plains, forests, rivers, seas and deserts, as well as man-made features like cities and larger political divisions such as city-states, kingdoms and conglomerates. The numerical designation following each entry refers to the principal scene or passage in which the entry is most prominently discussed. The Roman numerals I, II, III, and IV signify the volume of the Epic. "I" indicates the First Book, *The Warrior of World's End*, "II," *The Enchantress of World's End*, "III," *The Immortal of World's End*, and "IV," *The Barbarian of World's End*. The Arabic numeral identifies the specific chapter of the book in which the name occurs. The first portion of the Glossary appeared in *The Immortal of World's End*.

* * *

KAJJA. A Malme River city, inhabited by Voygych. IV, 16.
KAKKAWAKKA ISLANDS. Jungle isles, inhabited by savages, situated in the Sea of Zelphodon in Southern YamaYamaLand. I, 3.

KAN ZAR KAN. A mobile city, relic of the Vandkalexians, self-cognizant, self-animate, and situated in the Purple Plains. At the period of Ganelon's visit, the robot realm was inhabited by gypsylike Iomagoths. II, 22 and thereon.

KARCHOY. A city-state in the southeastern corner of Gondwane, ruled by the magician Zelobian. Ganelon does not reach Karchoy until the Eighth Book, but it is mentioned early on. II, *Appendix:* "Magic."

KARJIXIA. The country of the Tigermen in Northern YamaYamaLand. The capital is Xombol and the monarch regnant at the time of Silvermane's first visit to that realm was Prince Vrowl. I, 18.

KASHPODE. A city in the Merdingian Regnate of Upper Arzenia.

KHOND. Land of the Warrior Women, a sort of Amazon race, in the northern parts of Lesser Zuavia. I, 19.

KLISH. A region east of Yombok, in Lesser Zuavia, famous as the site of the Shrine of the Floating Stones, sacred to the religion of the Zealots of Jashp. II, 24.

KURUZ. A beautiful city to the north of the Iriboth Mountains of Greater Zuavia, where the men wear veils of mauve gauze and the women wear nothing at all. Despite its luxuriance, Kuruz is known as the least hospitable of all cities. III, 17.

LABRYS. One of the northernmost of the Thirty Cities of Gompia, guarding the Vigola Pass. IV, 11.

LAKE PARGE. Watery home of the Great God Glugluck. IV, 18.

LAND OF THE DEAD CITIES. A locale in Southern YamaYamaLand, also known as Caostro (which see). I, 3.

LAND OF RED MAGIC. A barren and little-inhabited region directly to the north of the Hegemony, ruled by Zelmarine the notorious Red Enchantress from her newly built capital, Shai. II, 8.

THE LARGROOLIAN PLAINS. A tropic region of Southern YamaYamaLand, bounded to the west by the Smoking Mountains. I, 3.

LEMMERY. One of the Empty Cities of Malme River Country. IV, 16.

THE LESSER POMMERNARIAN SEA. Really only a medium-to-smallish lake, this inland body of water was declared an inland sea by direct fiat of Agzan, the Phophet of Iksk. Both the Lesser Sea, and the Greater Sea to the north, derive their name from Pommernar, the original jumping-off-place from which Agzan led the Pommernarian Migration. III, 17.

LESSER ZUAVIA. A Conglomerate to the east of Greater Zuavia. It also borders on the Purple Plains, and contains Xoroth the Fire Desert, as well as the realms of the famous Tensors of Pluron. II, *Appendix:* "Greater Zuavia."

LUZ. A twi-horned peak at the western terminus of the Mountains of the Death Dwarves; at Mount Luz, Ganelon and his companions were nearly ambushed after traversing the Voormish Desert in the Flying Bazonga. I, 15.

LUZAR PASS. The only passageway through the Carthazian Mountains, permitting the traveler to cross from Valardus into Nimboland. III, 4.

LUZZUMA. One of the Thirty Cities, guarding the Pergode Pass. It was while returning to Luzzuma that Ganelon Silvermane was ambushed by Black Unggo. IV, 7.

LYZASH. A country of Upper Arzenia, to the north of Pardoga; the famous Warzoon, called the "City of Magicians," is situated in that country. IV, 14.

MALME RIVER COUNTRY. A deserted country beyond the Marvelous Mountains in Upper Arzenia. IV, 16.

MANTRAGON. In the remote past, a region near Trantain, home of the celebrated Pluralist of Mantragon. I, 8.

MARMORANAX. According to the Zul-and-Rashemba Mythos, a Cosmic Mountain at the very center of Gondwane. A palace on its crest, formerly the divine abode of the original Gods of the Mythos, is now the residence of Galendil the Good. I, *Appendix:* "Zul-and-Rashemba Mythos."

THE MARVELOUS MOUNTAINS. A range of pure lapis lazuli, in Upper Arzenia, marvelously sculpted by the Artisans of Zed. IV, 16.

MERDINGIAN REGNATE. A country in Upper Arzenia where the Ximchak Horde finally disbanded and settled down.

MONOSYLLABIC EMPIRE. A major nation in Northern
YamaYamaLand, believed to have flourished in the early
millennia of Ganelon's Eon, and to have disintegrated
into its component states of Chx, Ning, Quay, Horx,
Poy, Cham, and (possibly) Ixland. II, *Appendix:* "Chx."

MOUNTAINS OF THE DEATH DWARVES. Forming the
spine of Dwarfland, this range runs from east to west between Horx and the Great Chasm of Ygg. II, 15.

MOUNT ZIPHPHIZ. A volcanic peak in Garongaland inhabited by communities of hermits. I, 3.

MUNGDA. A Gompish city to the north of Jurago. IV, 7.

NAMBALOTH. One of the nine cities of the Hegemony. I,
3.

NAROOB. The mountain in Greater Zuavia atop which
Palensus Choy resides in his palace of Zaradon. III, 10.

NEMBOSCH. An important metropolis in Southern YamaYamaLand, home of the famous College of the Sixty
Sciences. I, 11.

NERELON. The enchanted palace of the famous celebrated
Illusionist, situated in the Crystal Mountains. I, 10.

NIMBOLAND. A jungle country north of the Carthazians,
inhabited by a race of vegetarian pacifists. Their monarch
is King Wunx, their capital a town called Urchak. III, 9.

NIMBO RIVER. A stream which descends from the Iriboth
Mountains and flows south through Nimboland. III, 9.

NING. A desolate country between Poy and Ixland, home of
a cult called the Mentalists of Ning. Queen Zelmarine
kept a Ningevite Mentalist in her court at Shai. II, 1.
et seq.

NYGOSH. One of the Merdingian cities, at war with
Spoyda at the time Ganelon led the Ximchaks into that
region.

ONG. A grassy region north of Trancore, inhabited by Hoppers. IV, 12.

ONGONOGA. A jungle country in Southern YamaYamaLand, home of the Great White Youk, which also in-
habits the Purple Plains. I, 12.

ONGADONGA MOUNTAINS. A range forming a natural
barrier between Ong and Posch. IV, 12.

ORDOVOY. A small, peaceful country bordering on Nimboland to the east. III, 9.

ORYX. A city in the center of the Hegemony, which serves
that realm in lieu of a formal capital. I, 3.

OTH-YOM-BARQA. A city-state in Southern YamaYamaLand in whose hills are found a species of sentient
crystalloids. Birthplace of Phlesco the Godmaker, Ganelon's foster-father. I, 2.

THE OVARVA PLAINS. A level grassland due east of
Trancore through which the Wryneck meanders. Scene
of a famous battle in which Flying Castle decimated the
Ximchak forces attempting to lay siege to the capital of
the Gray Dynasts. III, 24.

OYM. A city or nation forgotten in time, save that it was
home to the renegade sorcerer, Langarch. I, 11.

PARDOGA. A rocky country living in terror of the Strange
Little Men of the Hills.

PARVANIA. I don't know anything at all about Parvania.
It's down here in my notes, but, frankly, I can't remember where in the first four books of the Epic it's mentioned. The hell with Parvania, anyway.

PATHON THAD. Walled city of weaver-folk on an island
amidst Lake Xor in westernmost Greater Zuavia. IV, 12.

PERGAMOY. One of the cities of the Hegemony, north of
Zermish. I, 3.

PESH. A theocratic state devoted to the worship of the
Twelve Mysteries, and governed by the Mysteriarchs. II,
13.

PHEX. The extinct civilization of the Phexians dwelt around
the Crystal Mountains in Northern YamaYamaLand, before they perished in the Laughing Plague half an Eon
before the time of Ganelon Silvermane. I, 1.

PHOY. A distant realm with which the Zermishmen traded.
I, 3.

PHRENE. A river in the Malmanian country, scene of a
battle with the Voygych River Brigands. IV, 16.

PHYNX. A country north of Karjixia through which the Indigons traveled south. I, 4.

PLAINS OF UTH. Meadowlands due west of Zermish, site
of Ganelon's famous victory against the abovementioned
Indigons. I, 6.

PLAINS OF VLAD. A region in the northwestern parts of
Gondwane, beyond which Vandalex flourished. Ganelon

is to visit these Plains and encounter the Prairie Pirates in the Eighth Book of the Epic. I, *Appendix:* "Vandalex."

PLURON. A country lost in the haze of remotest history, where the famous Tensors of Pluron reigned, concerning whom little is known. II, 13, and elsewhere.

POMMERNARIAN SEAS. There are two of them, the Greater and the Lesser, and both are in Greater Zuavia. III, 17.

PORCHAVOY. A country of Upper Arzenia, north of which the Horde passed on its Great Migration. IV, 12.

PORT OYJ. Originally an island city in the Lost Sea of Voorm, now a city atop a mesa surrounded by the Voormish Desert, which is the dead sea-bottom of that same inland ocean. I, 16.

POSCH. A meadowland west of the Ongadonga Mountains and north of Trancore, inhabited by game birds, flying fish, and a peculiar species of perambulating vegetables. IV, 12.

POY. A small country north of the Land of Red Magic, beyond the Mountains of the Death Dwarves. II, *Appendix:* "Chx."

QOY. An arboreal region of Greater Zuavia, traversed by the Xorish River, inhabited by a race of Foresters. IV, 12.

QUAY. A country north of Ixland, south of Yombok, in Northern YamaYamaLand. I, 4, and elsewhere.

QUEE. A kingdom in the Badlands of Upper Arzenia. IV, 12.

QUENTLAND. Homeland of the Fabricators of Dirdanx. I, 9.

QUONSECA. A distant region from which the Urghazkoy arose to lead the Green Jehad. I, 10.

QUOYD. A sacred city in Upper Arzenia, inhabited mostly by priests. IV, 16.

To be continued in the next book of this series.

Presenting JOHN NORMAN in DAW editions . . .

☐ **SLAVE GIRL OF GOR.** The eleventh novel of Earth's orbital counterpart makes an Earth girl a puppet of vast conflicting forces. The 1977 Gor novel.   (#UJ1285—$1.95)

☐ **TRIBESMEN OF GOR.** The tenth novel of Tarl Cabot takes him face to face with the Others' most dangerous plot—in the vast Tahari desert with its warring tribes.
(#UE1296—$1.75)

☐ **HUNTERS OF GOR.** The saga of Tarl Cabot on Earth's orbital counterpart reaches a climax as Tarl seeks his lost Talena among the outlaws and panther women of the wilderness.   (#UE1294—$1.75)

☐ **MARAUDERS OF GOR.** The ninth novel of Tarl Cabot's adventures takes him to the northland of transplanted Vikings and into direct confrontation with the enemies of two worlds.   (#UE1295—$1.75)

☐ **TIME SLAVE.** The creator of Gor brings back the days of the caveman in a vivid lusty new novel of time travel and human destiny.   (#UW1204—$1.50)

☐ **IMAGINATIVE SEX.** A study of the sexuality of male and female which leads to a new revelation of sensual liberation.   (#UJ1146—$1.95)

DAW BOOKS are represented by the publishers of Signet and Mentor Books, **THE NEW AMERICAN LIBRARY, INC.**

THE NEW AMERICAN LIBRARY, INC.,
P.O. Box 999, Bergenfield, New Jersey 07621

Please send me the DAW BOOKS I have checked above. I am enclosing $_____(check or money order—no currency or C.O.D.'s). Please include the list price plus 35¢ a copy to cover mailing costs.

Name_____

Address_____

City_____State_____Zip Code_____
Please allow at least 4 weeks for delivery

Lin Carter's bestselling series!

☐ **UNDER THE GREEN STAR.** A marvel adventure in the grand tradition of Burroughs and Merritt. Book I.
(#UY1185—$1.25)

☐ **WHEN THE GREEN STAR CALLS.** Beyond Mars shines the beacon of exotic adventure. Book II. (#UY1267—$1.25)

☐ **BY THE LIGHT OF THE GREEN STAR.** Lost amid the giant trees, nothing daunted his search for his princess and her crown. Book III. (#UY1268—$1.25)

☐ **AS THE GREEN STAR RISES.** Adrift on the uncharted sea of a nameless world, hope still burned bright. Book IV.
(#UY1156—$1.25)

☐ **IN THE GREEN STAR'S GLOW.** The grand climax of an adventure amid monsters and marvels of a far-off world. Book V. (#UY1216—$1.25)

DAW BOOKS are represented by the publishers of Signet and Mentor Books, **THE NEW AMERICAN LIBRARY, INC.**

THE NEW AMERICAN LIBRARY, INC.,
P.O. Box 999, Bergenfield, New Jersey 07621

Please send me the DAW BOOKS I have checked above. I am enclosing
$_____(check or money order—no currency or C.O.D.'s).
Please include the list price plus 35¢ a copy to cover mailing costs.

Name_____

Address_____

City_____State_____Zip Code_____
Please allow at least 4 weeks for delivery

ALAN BURT AKERS

Six terrific novels compose the second great series
of adventure of Dray Prescot: The Havilfar Cycle.

☐ **MANHOUNDS OF ANTARES.** Dray Prescot on the unknown continent of Havilfar seeks the secret of the air-
boats. Book VI. (#UY1124—$1.25)

☐ **ARENA OF ANTARES.** Prescot confronts strange beasts
and fiercer men on that enemy continent. Book VII.
(#UY1145—$1.25)

☐ **FLIERS OF ANTARES.** In the very heart of his enemies,
Prescot roots out the secrets of flying. Book VIII.
(#UY1165—$1.25)

☐ **BLADESMAN OF ANTARES.** King or slave? Savior or be-
trayer? Prescot confronts his choices. Book IX.
(#UY1188—$1.25)

☐ **AVENGER OF ANTARES.** Prescot must fight for his enemies in order to save his friends! Book X.
(#UY1208—$1.25)

☐ **ARMADA OF ANTARES.** All the forces of two continents
mass for the final showdown with Havilfar's ambitious
queen. Book XI. (#UY1227—$1.25)

DAW BOOKS are represented by the publishers of Signet
and Mentor Books, **THE NEW AMERICAN LIBRARY, INC.**

THE NEW AMERICAN LIBRARY, INC.,
P.O. Box 999, Bergenfield, New Jersey 07621

Please send me the DAW BOOKS I have checked above. I am enclosing
$_____(check or money order—no currency or C.O.D.'s).
Please include the list price plus 35¢ a copy to cover mailing costs.

Name_____

Address_____

City_____State_____Zip Code_____
Please allow at least 4 weeks for delivery

DAW≡sf BOOKS

☐ **ELRIC OF MELNIBONE by Michael Moorcock.** The first of the great sagas of the Eternal Champion—back in print in a new and corrected edition. (#UY1259—$1.25)

☐ **THE SAILOR ON THE SEAS OF FATE by Michael Moorcock.** The second Elric novel—now first published in America. (#UY1270—$1.25)

☐ **LEGENDS FROM THE END OF TIME by Michael Moorcock.** Strange and diverting adventures of the last decadents on Earth. (#UY1281—$1.25)

☐ **THE JEWEL IN THE SKULL by Michael Moorcock.** The First Book in the History of the Runestaff. (#UY1276—$1.25)

☐ **THE WEIRD OF THE WHITE WOLF by Michael Moorcock.** The third novel of the saga of Elric of Melnibone. (#UY1286—$1.25)

☐ **THE MAD GOD'S AMULET by Michael Moorcock.** The second Book in the History of the Runestaff. (#UY1289—$1.25)

☐ **THE LAND LEVIATHAN by Michael Moorcock.** High adventure in an alternate past and an alternate future. (#UY1214—$1.25)

DAW BOOKS are represented by the publishers of Signet and Mentor Books, THE NEW AMERICAN LIBRARY, INC.

THE NEW AMERICAN LIBRARY, INC.,
P.O. Box 999, Bergenfield, New Jersey 07621

Please send me the DAW BOOKS I have checked above. I am enclosing
$_____(check or money order—no currency or C.O.D.'s).
Please include the list price plus 35¢ a copy to cover mailing costs.

Name_____

Address_____

City_____State_____Zip Code_____
Please allow at least 4 weeks for delivery